CALL ME
JAZZY

CARLA STEWART

Published in the United States of America by:

Divine-Publishing
3021 Thrasher Circle
Atlanta, GA 30032

www.divinely-chosen.com

DEDICATION

To my sons who once believed I could do anything, and my Mainstreet Girls, especially Jackie, who died of breast cancer. I will love you guys forever.

ACKNOWLEDGEMENT

The author would like to acknowledge the help of the following people: Armond Jenkins, youngest offspring, engineer, computer technology support; Cora Lima, retired English teacher, media specialist; Jackie Carter, author, retired educator, world traveler; Anita Clay, author, retired educator; Olive Lewis, author, publisher; Ann Hunt-Smith, author, editor; and The Lou Walker Writer's Guild.

PROLOGUE

Was the answer to my life long dilemma standing on the opposite side of the glass window? That is the question I had been wondering for a long time. At this juncture now my heart is screaming yes, yes, yes, but my mind is saying no, no, no! Should I follow my mind or what I feel in my heart?

My name is Jazmine Walton, but my family and friends call me Jazzy. I enjoy working for my advertising agency in Atlanta, Georgia. Not only am I incredibly skilled, because I earned a marketing degree from a prestigious Texas university but also from hard lessons learned during my youth.

I am an attractive woman with a fit body and long, curly, reddish-brown hair. I meet with a trainer at a gym three times a week and run at the park the other days. As a child, exercise helped to keep my mind alert, and my body tight. I learned the importance of training from my father. The only quality time spent with my dad was on our early morning jogs near our home in southern Louisiana.

I love the world of advertising. As co-owner of an advertising agency, it takes charm and talent to convince clients to rely on our agency to create their commercials and print ads. I have an abundance of both. It is also our job to help our clients increase their company's profits. Our client base is growing steadily.

I work seriously long hours. When I'm working, I feel alive and appreciated. Sometimes, my work leads me to exciting and exotic places all over the world. I always travel in the company of others, because I detest traveling alone. I meet with friends several times for dinner or drinks because I enjoy their company.

Now and then, I go out on dates, but my relationships with the opposite sex never last very long. For the most part, I usually remain friends with the men I date. Since the majority of them are professional men, they are always an excellent source for business advice.

I have had a few infatuations over time, but I never seem to find the real thing. I'm referring to unconditional love. However, I am too busy to worry about any of that because I am presently living my best life. I work hard but play hard also.

Sometimes, it feels as though I'm two different people. At work, I am "Ms. Jazmine Walton" a successful career woman. When I play, I am "Jazzy," wild and free. "Jazmine" of the advertising world is bold, beautiful, charming, and deadly in business. However, the fun-loving, "Jazzy" is a little insecure, and longs for the approval of her critical father.

Outwardly, it appears that I have everything. Even though I run a successful business and have enough money to buy anything my heart desires, it feels as though something is missing. I have no clue what that something is, and I am not even sure it exists. If it does, I am bound and determined to find it someday.

ONE

The night we met, I felt an instant attraction. I had never felt that way about a man before, so what I was feeling was very foreign. My body felt warm and tingly all over, and my heart was humming a tune I had never heard before. Since I was feeling flushed, I guess I was blushing. What was happening to me? I wondered.

Unfortunately, he was an engaged man. Ironically, I had recently met his fiancé a couple of weeks before at the shopping mall. I was a cashier at the movie theater for the summer before I left for college. It was my first job. I was eighteen years old.

It surprised me to see her again, but there they were, at the counter, waiting to buy movie tickets.

"Hello," she said. "I know you are Cathy's cousin, but I forgot your name." Then she interjected, "This is my fiancé."

"Hey," I said in return. "How are you guys doing?"

He reached out to shake my hand and said, "Hello, young lady. My name is Paul Huntly. What is your name?"

"My name is Jazmine," I answered with a smile as I reached to shake his hand. It felt warm, and I didn't want to let it go. That was very odd for me too, but nothing felt normal that night.

He was so handsome and seemed friendly, with a bright, genuine smile. With his muscular body, it was easy to see he worked out a lot.

"Pleased to meet you, Jazzy," he said and laughed.

I had to quickly pull my hand away from him because his fiancé began to glare.

During the following weeks, they came back to the theater a few more times and seemed happy together.

A couple of weeks after we met, something happened that changed my life forever. "OMG," I thought. I spotted Paul walking down the sidewalk near the entrance to our town's most popular night club. He was accompanying an attractive woman.

I was sitting in the backseat of my girlfriend, Dianne's car. It was Saturday night, and traffic was moving slowly on that one-way street. I watched as he laughed and talked with the woman as they inched closer to the head of the long line of the club.

"That is not his fiancé," I thought to myself as I wondered where she was and why they weren't together.

I had never seen the two of them apart, except for the visits he made to purchase snacks at the concession stand. Even though he bought a lot of junk food, I never saw him eat any. I didn't understand why he bought so much, and I could never tell if he was flirting with me or not. He smiled a lot and made me laugh, and that was pretty much all I remembered. He was always polite and never said anything inappropriate.

Dianne finally found a place to park her car. She and my other two companions refreshed their lipstick and joined me in the long line at the club's entrance. It only took a few minutes. We used our fake ID cards and paid the admission price to enter the popular nightspot. I didn't like alcohol, but I loved the sound of music, dancing and meeting new people.

I quickly began to look around the club for Paul. After a short while, I spotted him on the dance floor. To my amazement, he was not dancing with his fiancé or the woman who accompanied him on the sidewalk. I did not see the woman he was engaged to anywhere.

As I continued to look around, he spotted me. After he left the dance floor, he walked over to where I was standing.

"Hello Jazzy. Is that you? What are you doing here?"

I was extremely nervous standing so close to him, but finally managed to say,

"I'm great! How are you doing?" Little did he know, I was feeling excited because I had just located him on the dance floor! "I just left a concert with my girlfriends, and we stopped here to party before we go home." Then, I finally asked him the question I had been dying to ask. "Where is your fiancé tonight? I didn't see her? Is she okay?"

"We split up, and she moved back home to her parent's house. Then he quickly changed the subject. "Would you like to dance Jazzy? The DJ is playing one of my favorite songs!"

I nodded yes because I could not speak. My tongue seemed to stick in my mouth. He took my hand and guided me to the dance floor. I was so excited because this fine man had asked me to dance.

After we danced to a couple of songs, he offered to buy me a drink. Since I did not want any alcohol, I asked for a bottle of water. He ordered water for both of us. He said he didn't drink alcohol either.

"So, beautiful lady, are you enjoying yourself this wonderful evening?" He asked.

"Yes, I'm having a great time. What about you? Thanks for the water."

"I am having a fantastic time with you!" was his reply. This time, I could tell he was flirting, and I giggled.

"The concert at the Hampton Civic Center tonight was awesome. My girlfriends and I enjoyed the band so much. I am hoarse from screaming,"

I mentioned this just to keep a dialogue going. He smelled wonderful and was even more muscular than I thought. We talked and danced for hours. During our conversation, we discovered that we had something in common. Paul and I had been abandoned by our mothers, leaving a missing piece in our hearts. We did not view that fact the same.

My mother died when I was a baby. His mother abandoned him, along with his brothers and sisters, after his parent's divorce. He was the youngest when she moved away. Paul's father, along with his grandmother's help, raised them. She lived a mile away from them. This beautiful man never wanted to meet his mother. He never forgave her for leaving them.

My mom has passed away; his mother chose to walk away. Paul had no memories of her and no desire to spend time with his mother. I longed to see my mother almost every day, but I will never have that chance. Even though he tried to explain, my longing would not allow me to understand why he would not reach out to his mother.

"Papa was wonderful to me, and he was all I needed. I loved him very much. My dad filled the role of both parents, so I did not need for her in my life, he said, as he changed the subject again.

Would you like to dance one more time? It is close to the time for this club to close."

How could I refuse one last slow dance in his strong arms?

"Yes," I said. I reached out my hand and we headed back to the dance floor.

As the evening was coming to an end, he offered me a ride home. I found my girlfriend, Diane, on the dance floor and told her I had a ride home with the guy I had been mentioning.

"I thought you told me he is engaged to be married soon." she exclaimed, with an emphasis on the word engaged.

"They broke up," I whispered into her ear. I smiled as I walked away.

"Call me tomorrow, girl!" she said. "I want to hear all about it."

Paul drove me home and walked me to my front door. "Would you like to go to a cookout with me Sunday afternoon?" he asked.

Trying hard not to sound as excited as I felt, I replied, "Sure, I would love to go with you!"

He kissed me sweetly on the cheek and said, "Good night, young lady. I will call you tomorrow."

"Goodbye. I had a great time tonight. I'll look forward to your call tomorrow."

Paul had changed the subject whenever he finished talking about something he didn't like. To me, that was not such a big deal. I was accustomed to it because my father communicated with me the same way. Other than that, he had been the perfect gentleman Just like the handsome prince or knight in shining armor little girls read about in fairy tales. My view of him was through rose-colored glasses. I was young, barely eighteen, but convinced I was ready for romance. I believed I had found the one, but we all know that real life is not a fairy tale.

TWO

Paul picked me up on Sunday at 4:00 p.m. I liked the fact that he was punctual. I was so excited; I would have waited on him for any length of time. We headed to one of his cousin's apartment. When we walked in, a football game was blaring on a widescreen television. The meat was cooking on a large grill; it smelled great. There was food everywhere. The apartment was full of his cousins and friends, both male and female.

"Hey guys, this is my friend Jazzy."

"Hello everyone," I said shyly, as they all greeted me with welcoming smiles.

I noticed that Paul wasn't drinking any alcoholic beverages, nor smoking whatever they were passing around. They were talking loudly about sports, but their conversations were friendly. Since they had grown up around each other, they seemed to be a very close-knit group. The majority of them worked at the same company. I considered that Sunday to be our first date. It was a beautiful day.

My new love taught me how to live life to the fullest. We did a lot of things together that summer before I left my first year of college. We went to parties, movies, concerts, and picnics in the park.

He introduced me to a world of pleasure I had never known before. That was the summer I became a woman, because he slowly and gently introduced me to the art of making love. Before we met, I had never been intimate with a man. We were very much in love.

He never wanted to talk about marriage, so that subject was always off the table. Marrying him was still on my mind. One of his cousins informed me that Paul caught his fiancé in bed with another woman.

He was embarrassed, hurt, and felt betrayed. He refused to talk about it and acted as though it never happened, but I knew that the pain affected him. I guess he thought, "What is the point of getting close enough to discuss marriage. Jazzy is young and will be leaving soon for college."

Sometimes it made me a little sad. I dreamed of our future together almost every night. My plan was to move back to Louisiana after graduation, marry him, and start a family. We were not on the same page. Even though I knew he loved me, he wanted something different. He only wanted us to enjoy every free moment we had together before I left. Except for that one thing, my summer was the greatest joy I had ever known.

I was an inexperienced teenager; he was almost a decade older. I believe this was part of the reason my father didn't like him. He was not fond of anyone.

On the other hand, my grandmother loved Paul. Whenever he picked me up for a date; he brought her fresh flowers. It always made her smile. We were the perfect couple, so happy together. How could anything ever go wrong?

Unfortunately, we live in an imperfect world. Everything was fantastic until the "Proverbial" other shoe dropped.

THREE

After a few months of dating, one Saturday night, Paul called and said, "Hey Jazzy, I am driving my cousin to New Orleans to see his kids. He started drinking heavily when his wife moved back there to her parent's house. Of course, she took their children with her. I am afraid he is going to hurt himself or someone else."

I got bored waiting for him to call me back. My girlfriend, Dianne, called and asked me to take a ride with her. She was going to search for her boyfriend because she thought that he was cheating on her. He had cheated on her before, and she was determined to catch him in the act. Our first stop was at a bar downtown. We went to look around for her man, but we didn't find him.

However, I did find the love of my life, Paul, at the bar. His cousin was with him. They did not go to New Orleans, I thought! Three attractive women were sitting at the table next to them. Their tables and chairs were very close together. The women were laughing and flirting, but Paul was just sitting in his chair, smiling.

I stood there, frozen in my tracks, unable to move or speak. I continued watching for a while. He had no clue I was standing there. He never saw me, and fortunately, Diane did not see him. I could not believe my eyes nor identify my feelings. I was vacillating somewhere between rage and despair. I felt a sense of betrayal.

I left the bar with my girlfriend and didn't tell her what I had witnessed. I tried hard to keep a straight face all the way home. However, as soon as she drove me back to my house, the pain I felt was indescribable!

I awoke before the sun came up. I thought, "I can't sleep, can't eat or think clearly. I can barely breathe. I am void of tears because I have cried a river all night. What the hell am I going to do now? After the sun rose, I drove Nana's car to Paul's apartment and started yelling at him like a person possessed! "I saw you and your cousin at the bar with those women last night! You lied to me! You said you were taking him to New Orleans to see his wife and kids!"

I was enraged! As far as I was concerned, he had destroyed my trust. I was hurting; therefore, I refused to give him a chance to explain what happened. I stormed out of his apartment and never looked back.

The evening, after I broke up with him, Paul came to our house. Even though he knew my father did not like him, he walked up to the front door and rang our doorbell. Since I had walked out on him without allowing him to speak, he was determined to have his say. I had denied him that opportunity. Nana answered the door. She said, "Hello, young man. May I help you?"

"I am sorry to bother you, ma'am. May I please speak to Jazzy?" Paul requested.

Nana replied: "I'm not sure about that. What happened between the two of you? She is distraught with you, and won't come out of her room. She has not eaten anything today. I tried to convince her to eat a little soup this afternoon. When I took it into her room, she was in bed, but her eyes were red and swollen from crying."

"Yes ma'am. I know she is upset with me, but I have not done anything wrong. I need to explain to her what happened. I don't know what she thinks she saw last night, but I desperately need to talk to her about it. She stormed out of my apartment, screaming at the top of her lungs. I have never seen her behave like that before. I've called her several times today, but my messages are going straight to her voicemail! She has convinced herself that I lied, and she thinks that I am cheating with another woman. The only thing I did was I smile and say hello to those women. Cheating was the farthest thing from my mind. I love her. Jazzy just got the wrong impression of what happened." Paul continued to tell Nana his side of the incident.

"I told her earlier yesterday that my cousin needed me to drive him someplace, and I did. He had been drinking all day! I said I would call her when we returned. I took him to New Orleans to see his wife and kids. She refused to allow him to see his children because he was drunk. On our way back, he begged me to stop for a beer. I reluctantly said yes, and forgot to call Jazzy. In hindsight, I should have called to let her know the change in plans, but it was very late. I realize now that it was a terrible mistake. I should have taken my cousin straight home. Somehow, Jazzy saw us. I never thought she could ever get so angry with me about anything. He sighed heavily. Ms. Nana, I swear to you I would never do anything to hurt your granddaughter. When she stormed out of my apartment, she said that she never wanted to see me again. I don't know what to do."

"Young man, I am so sorry for the hurt you are both experiencing right now. She told me the same thing, and she doesn't want to see you. I must respect my granddaughter's decision. I wish I could do more to help you. I will try to talk to her again in the morning. Her father will be returning soon. He would become angry to see you here. I think you should go on home now. I promise I will relay your messages to her. Nana said, Goodnight."

"Thank you," Paul responded. He left our house feeling sad and rejected.

I never heard his explanation because I closed my door and started crying as soon as I heard Paul say hello to Nana. She came to my door and knocked softly. "That was your friend, Paul, at the door, Jazmine. He desperately wants to talk to you about what happened Saturday night. He said he has been trying to call you. Maybe you should listen to what he has to say."

Pausing for a few seconds, Nana continued to speak outside my door. "Are you ok, baby? Would you like Nana to bring you something to eat, or maybe some juice to drink? You know it worries me when you don't eat anything," She exclaimed.

"No, thank you. I will be okay. Please don't worry about me," I said.

"Okay, baby. Try and get some sleep," She said.

"Thank you, Nana. Goodnight," I replied through muffled tears. I wondered if I would ever be okay again. However, soon after, I drifted off to sleep.

The next day, I woke up hungry with a slight headache. I got out of bed, took a long hot shower, and washed my hair. The lovely floral scents lifted my spirits a little. I smelled bacon and Nana's homemade biscuits. I dressed quickly and went downstairs to breakfast.

Daddy was back from his business trip and was sitting at the table with a cup of coffee. He and Nana were talking. He took one look at me and asked, "Are you feeling okay, Jazmine? You look very pale, and your eyes are red. Are your allergies acting up again? Should you see the doctor before you leave for college tomorrow?"

"No, I feel fine. I'm just excited about going away to school. I didn't get much sleep last night. I was up late packing," I continued. I had been packing for college for weeks. My things were packed and ready for the trip.

Unfortunately, he wasn't listening. He was looking at his cell phone. Does he even care? I wondered.

"We should leave for Texas Friday at 9:00 am sharp. First, the car will pick you up here at the house. Then the driver will pick me up at the office. Someone at the security desk will inform me when you arrive," Daddy said. It was more of an order than a question, so Nana and I just shook our heads in agreement.

As soon as Daddy left for work, Nana attempted to approach the subject about what happened the previous night. She said, "Jasmine that young man was courageous to come here and try to make things right with you."

"I know," I said. Then I hugged Nana and told her I did not want to talk about it anymore. Finally, she stopped trying to change my mind. I never learned the truth about what happened that Saturday night. In retrospect, not listening to Paul's explanation was one of the biggest mistakes of my life.

I could hardly wait to go away to college and never come back home again. I had never experienced real pain before that fateful summer night. Nana and Daddy had always made sure of it. They had successfully protected me all my life from physical as well as emotional distress. I was unprepared for this calamity. No one on Earth could protect me from the pain of my first broken heart. He was my first love. I would never forget him.

FOUR

After leaving Jazmine's house, I felt so miserable. For the first time in and almost forever, I did not know what I was going to do. I was tired and felt drained of all my energy. I returned my apartment, took off my clothes, and crawled into bed. I quickly fell asleep.

The next day after work, I decided to have a talk with Papa. I head to the cemetery. I don't see anyone else near Papa's grave site, so I take a seat on the grass near his headstone. I began to talk. "Papa, I don't understand any of this. My heart is aching because it is broken into pieces. I love Jazmine so much but she won't talk to me. I know that if you were here; you would help me figure out what to do." I was planning to ask her to marry me, after she finished college. She didn't know that I wanted to spend the rest of my life with her, as my wife. I never told her how I felt; now it is too late! She won't even answer my calls. Please help me Papa figure out what to do."

I opened my eyes, noticed the beautiful blue sky, felt the cool breeze, and took a deep breath. I begin to feel a sense of calmness come over. It was such a lovely day. All of a sudden, I remember my Papa's words. "Paul, just give it a little more time. Everything will be okay." My father was a very wise man. I felt better after I left the cemetery. I wiped away the tears from my eyes, straighten my back, and headed home.

I thought, Jazmine would be leaving soon for college. Even though I loved her with all my heart, she was young and had her whole life ahead of her. I prayed that she would have a happy life. I needed something else in my life to ease my pain. After I reached my apartment, I fell asleep. I slept the entire afternoon and did not wake up until morning. My first thought was of Jazmine, and then I remembered the pain. Maybe I should write her a letter? Then, I thought better of it and asked myself, "What good would that do?" I had left so many messages for her. She was stubborn. Jazmine had made up her mind that I was cheating on her. I didn't want to think about how much pain she must be feeling also. I tried hard to free my mind. I got up, showered, got dressed, and headed to work.

I had been saving money, for a long time, to start my own construction company. It was the best time for me to pursue my life-long dream. I needed to focus all my attention on something positive. My great-uncle was getting old and wanted to sell his construction tools and equipment. We negotiated on a price and worked out a contract. I gave him a down payment and he allowed me to pay off the balance in three years' time. In order to look like a serious business owner, I had my hair cut very short and shaved off my beard. Since, I had a cleanly shaven face, my dimples were more noticeable. That better enhanced my smile.

A few years later, my first large construction bid was for a large contract was Company. Mr. Walton, Jazmine's father, accepted my bid. He didn't recognize me. I guess that was great for both of us. I was amazed when I found out about the acceptance of the bid. I was determined to make him proud of me, even though he had no clue that I was Jazmine's old boyfriend.

He exclaimed. "Son, that's what he called me, I chose your bid because it was not high or too low. It was somewhere in the middle. It was also the exact price that I allocated for this project. I guess this was meant to be."

My small crew had completed many small jobs before but nothing of this magnitude. We would be building townhouses in a small gated community. The work-site was in the town next to one where I lived. I would be a short commute to work every day. I looked forward to working. It seemed to be the only thing in my life I had to look forward too.

Since Jazmine and I had broken up, I had been approached by several women. They flirted and carried on, but I never found anyone I was interested in dating. Once, my cousin, Wanda introduced me to one of her sorority sisters. She set up blind date for us to meet at a local café. She was lovely woman. She had a decent conversation. We dated for a few months. However, we agreed, around the same time, that we would be better suited for dating other people. We parted amicably.

After that relationship ended, I focused totally on my construction company. I decided that I needed a dog to keep me company in the evenings. I was always lonely at night. I decided to adopt a golden retriever puppy from the local animal shelter. I named him Goldie. I had already moved into a house. It was a small ranch style home that needed a lot of remodeling. At least now, both my puppy and my new home gave me something to look forward to every evening. My retriever was always happy to see me when I returned from work. As soon as the front door opened, he would jump straight into my arms. As he got older and much larger, he would wait at the front door with his leash in his mouth. He needed to go outside, take care of his doggy business, and run around for a while in the yard.

After our daily walks, I would spend time completing small projects inside my house. It had three bedrooms, nothing fabulous, and the only thing that worked in the kitchen was the stove. I didn't cook much.

I had an awesome patio with a large smoker, grill. I used it mostly to cook my meals. My dog and I spent our evenings on the patio. After dinner, I gazed at the stars. I didn't care much for television shows and the news with always so discouraging. I very rarely watched. Sometimes, when I was very lonely, I would allow myself sweet memories of Jazmine. In my mind, I remembered her laughing, making funny jokes, and pushing up next to me. We had spent a lot of time together. I wondered what she was up to at the present time. I didn't have to wait very long to find out.

Early one morning, Mr. Walton came to the work site to check on the progress of the townhouses. We had completed one of them, and we were near completion of the others. He wanted to check with me to see how much progress my crew had made. He had been at the work site twice before. On this particular day, he said. "Young people are really doing well in business these days. I have a daughter that just started her own business also. She and a partner opened an advertising agency in Atlanta, GA. She is always very busy and never comes home anymore. Sometimes, I wonder if I am the reason she stays away. I was very hard on her when she was young. I miss her a lot. I am very proud of her, and you too Son. I took a chance on you and you have not proved my wrong."

"Mr. Walton, have you ever told your daughter how you feel about her?"

"No, not really, maybe I will someday. However, right now, I want to walk through your first completed townhouse. That is why I am here this morning. I want to have a good look at everything. A few couples have contacted the office to inquire about the prices of these homes. One young couple asked if they could put in an offer to buy one of these townhouses. I told them there offer it was a bit premature. Now that I see how much progress you have made, I will call them back. I kept their numbers and told them I would be in touch soon."

After our walk through the structures was complete, Mr. Walton exclaimed. "It is time for me to get back to my office. Everything here looks like it is in ship shape."

When my conversation with Mr. Walton was finished, I quickly decided to look on the web to see if I could find any information about Jazmine when I got home. I say to myself, "I will look on all the social media sights to find pictures of her." I thought surely she had grown into a beautiful woman.

As soon as I finished walking the dog, I headed straight to my office and turned on my computer, instead of heading out to the patio. My dog, Goldie, came over and put his head on my lap. I was quickly able to find pictures of Jazmine. After a few short clicks of the computer keys, she was very easy to find. "Wow! She is beautiful. Her hair is longer, but her face is the same. Her lips look like they are thicker than they were before. Her eyes are beautiful, and her smile is the same. She looks very happy," I exclaimed. I start to feel sad all over again. "Enough." I say to myself. "Let it go and get on with your life!" Goldie looks at me and whimpers. I turn off the computer and head outside to the patio.

FIVE

The following week I left for college. That painful week ended with Nana helping me decorate my new dormitory room for the start of my freshman year. When we arrived, my college roommate was already there with her mother, father, and two younger brothers. They seemed like a happy family unit, as they hugged and attempted to say goodbye. Her mother had tears streaming down her face. She tried very hard to remain courageous, but she was having a difficult time letting go of her baby girl. I had never witnessed that kind of emotion between family members. My heart was touched to see such strong a bond.

Nana cleared her throat and said, "Hello there."

They turned around and said, "Good morning." in unison, and introduced themselves to us.

My roommate said, "Hey, girl, my name is Tina. I am happy to meet you in person."

I said, "Hey," with a broad smile-feeling happy and ready to begin a new adventure.

That was the way I felt at that moment. However, I knew I was going to miss my Nana so much, but I was ready to experience the freedom of adult life. I planned to live my life of freedom and, hopefully, have a lot of fun!

When Nana and I finished setting up my half of the dorm room, we walked over to the building where Daddy was meeting with the president of the university. He never saw my room. He was anxious to get back on the road back to Louisiana.

We hugged goodbye at the car, and Nana held on to me for a very long time.

She whispered, "Be safe, my love and come home to visit us soon. I love you so much."

All my father managed to say was, "Call if you need anything. Nana and I need to be on our way." Then he gave me a quick peck on my cheek.

"Goodbye, I managed to say in a small voice. I love you guys."

The limousine driver opened car doors for him as well as Nana. She blew me a kiss from the car as it slowly pulled away from the curb. I was missing them both already before the vehicle reached the end of the lane. Then my tears began to flow.

I threw myself into my school work the first semester of my freshman year. It helped to distract me from the pain of losing my first love. I still felt so deeply hurt. In the beginning, I missed Paul so much. I thought of him every night before I drifted off to sleep.

Due to the fact that I focused so hard on my assignments, I made the dean's list both semesters of my freshman year. I only went home once that first year-during our Christmas break. I could not imagine the holidays without Nana.

My roommate, Tina, and I had become very close as soon as we met. She became like a sister to me. Daddy allowed me to go home with her for a few weeks during our first summer vacation. We had completed our first year of college, and we wanted to celebrate.

While I was visiting them, I witnessed how a happy family looks. They were all so kind to me. We had fun for several weeks, but

I missed my grandmother very much. I was ready to go home.

I called my father and told him I wanted to come home. I asked if I could bring my roommate, Tina, along. Her parents allowed her to go. Dad sent his driver to pick us up. That summer, Nana impressed Tina with her tasteful Cajun and Creole cooking. We both gained weight.

SIX

I began to enjoy college life a little more in my sophomore year. I started to relax a little and dated some of the guys on campus. I attended some Fraternity parties with Tina on the weekends.

Regretfully, the young men I dated could never compare to Paul. They seemed young and immature-more like boys. Learning about love from an older, wiser man had been a wonderful gift, and a curse all rolled into one.

My junior year was uneventful and passed by quickly. I started to feel more like an adult and felt ready to make decisions about my future. I decided I wanted to live in the southern region of the country, but I no longer wanted to move back to Louisiana to begin my career.

Before the end of the second semester of my junior year, I was offered a summer internship at a large advertising agency in Dallas, Texas. I had matured by then, so my father said he thought it was a good idea to accept their offer.

That was the summer I met Arden. He was a senior partner at the advertising agency. He was a tall sexy man with a broad chest. When he took off his jacket, you could see clearly that he worked out. He was well built and muscular. He had a perfect smile, the kind a woman could get lost in. Many women did just that. I had dated a few boys in college, but Arden seemed more like a real man. I was interested in learning more about him.

Soon after my internship began, one morning, we crossed paths in the hallway. "Hello, you are one of our new interns. Jazmine, right?" he questioned as he extended a hand. Then he introduced himself, "My name is Arden."

"Wow," I thought to myself, he remembered my name. "Yes, it is," I replied as I shook his hand. "My friends call me Jazzy."

"Okay Jazzy. I'm pleased to meet you, and I am looking forward to becoming good friends. How about we start building that new friendship on Friday night? Are you free for dinner?"

"Yes, I am free Friday night. I would like to find out whether we can become friends or not." I responded with a smile.

We bumped into each other again the following day in the break room. We both wanted a cup of coffee from the espresso machine. We smiled and said a friendly hello. After that, it seemed like a long time until our dinner date on Friday night.

I left work a little early on Thursday because I had appointments at the hair salon and my favorite nail shop. I was so busy preparing for the upcoming date that I forgot to eat dinner. I picked up a salad from a deli near my house and ate it while I watched a bit of the evening news. Afterward, I decided what I was going to wear on my highly anticipated date with Arden the following evening.

On Friday, we were both busy. I saw him once in the hallway near his office. He waved slightly and smiled. We agreed to meet after work at 6:30 p.m., near the bank of elevators, on the ground floor. I retrieved my garment bag from the closet at exactly 5:00 p.m. and went into the lady's room to get ready for our date.

The building was almost empty on Friday afternoon. I took my time getting dressed. I reapplied my makeup, brushed my hair, and changed into my favorite red dress. Afterward, I returned my bags to my car and headed to the elevators in the building.

Arden was punctual - a good trait in a man my father used to say. He stepped out of the elevator, looking as handsome as ever. He smelled divine.

"Hello Jazzy," he said with that dazzling smile. Then he asked, "How was your day?"

"A bit uneventful, I replied. How was yours?" I asked in return.

He exclaimed, "Actually, I had an awesome day. Our team sealed the deal on a new holiday campaign for one of our largest clients! We will be meeting for drinks around ten tonight. Would you like to join me and meet them after dinner? Have you met any senior members of our firm yet? It would be a great opportunity for a new intern. Are you interested?"

It was easy to see why he was such a successful advertising agent. He never accepted no for an answer.

Arden taught me many things that summer. Upon his recommendation, I was offered a position at the agency, beginning as soon as I completed my senior year.

I was excited about the career opportunity. I could not wait to share my good news with Nana and my father. My hopes were that my father would appreciate this great accomplishment.

At the beginning of my senior year, my roommate Tina moved into a house with her sorority sisters. She had pledged during our second year at the university. She had always been very popular on campus, not a shy, insecure nerd like me. I did not want a new roommate, so I begged Nana to help convince him that I was ready to move off-campus. He did not believe that I was mature enough to live alone, so he agreed to allow me to share an apartment with three other students. Maybe, he thought I was old enough to handle that. I didn't see Tina much that year. She spent the majority of her free time with her sorority sisters. They did not like me very much. I was not outgoing like Tina. I was always quiet and spent the majority of my time studying. For the most part, the year passed quickly and I enjoyed my last year at Texas State University worry free. Now, I could look forward to the position I had been offered, at the Dallas agency.

SEVEN

My career started at the largest and most prestigious advertising agency in Dallas, Texas. Fortunately, my assignment was to Arden's team. He had been my mentor, and we had remained friends. I was excited about my new job. I had learned a great deal about advertising during my summer internship.

At the end of my first year working in Texas, Arden married his high school sweetheart. It was a beautiful ceremony. I met her for the first time at one of our office parties. She was beautiful and very kind. It was impossible not to like her. Their families had been very close all their lives, so they grew up together. After they were married, his wife, Ashley, and I became close friends. They were expecting their first child. I believed that Arden would be a good father, one who would be loving and attentive to his children's needs.

Shortly after joining Arden's team, we started working on an international campaign for a famous sporting goods company. I enjoyed my work very much.

One morning, while supervising a photo-shoot for a print advertisement, one of the male models caught my attention. He looked up and glanced at me as I walked over to ask the photographer a question. He had tanned skinned, perfect teeth and a sexy close shaved beard. He even had dimples in his cheeks. Lucas Samuels was gorgeous and famous.

Following the photo-shoot, he handed me one of his business cards, then asked me to join him for dinner the following night. We exchanged cell numbers. I will give you a call, if I decide to meet you," I said softly.

Saturday night, bored with nothing better to do, I gave Lucas a call. I agreed to meet him for drinks instead of dinner. We decided to meet at a bar near my office building. It was very noisy at the bar, but we managed to have a decent conversation. He told me that he would be leaving the next morning for a photo in Paris, France. He said that he would be back in a few weeks, and also promised to give me a call when he got to Europe.

I didn't think much about it, but the following evening he gave me a call, and we talked for an hour. Lucas told me all about his photoshoot in Paris and sent me a few pictures from his cell phone. He was hilarious, and I enjoyed the way he made me laugh. Lucas promised to call after returning to Texas.

He did call me when he returned from Europe. This time we met for a nice dinner. I found him to be an interesting man. His conversations were intriguing. Besides being a gorgeous model, he was also intelligent and well-traveled.

We dated for more than a year, but his long-distance job assignments and my busy schedule made it hard to maintain a relationship. To this day, he is still one of the most famous models in the world. I continued to request him whenever the agency required a male model for commercials. We remained friends.

That relationship was the closest I had ever come to loving another man. After our dating relationship ended, I started to question if I was a damaged woman in the department of love. Lucas seemed like the perfect man, but not the perfect one for me.

At the end of years of working extremely long hours and weekends, I became one of the top-selling agents at the Texas agency. Under Arden's leadership, I had learned a great deal of information, but I knew it was time for a change.

Upon my thirtieth birthday, I inherited a substantial amount of money from my maternal grandfather, whom I had never met. Nana told me about the trust fund when I was younger. She explained that my mother was his only child.

I decided to use the money from my trust to start an advertising agency in Atlanta, Georgia. I convinced Arden and Ashley to join me in the new business venture. I also asked Arden to become a full partner in the new firm.

It took a bit of work to persuade Ashley to leave her family in Texas and move to Georgia. By that time, they had two young children. However, after a one week visit to the city of Atlanta, she was happy to make a move. Her parents, who were retired decided to move to Atlanta also; they wanted to be near their grandkids.

When Arden and I started our agency, a few of our former clients left the agency in Dallas and became our first clients. The name of our agency became J and A Advertising Agency. The J is for Jazmine, and the A from Arden and Ashley. Together they matched my funds to start the firm. Our small agency snowballed quickly, and we were successful. We were always busy with television commercials and print ads. By the end of our first year, we had hired ten new staff members.

EIGHT

A few years after we opened the agency in Atlanta, early one morning before a crucial presentation, I was about to leave my office and head towards our conference room. I felt a sharp pain in my chest and started to sweat. I sat down in a chair for a few minutes, took a deep breath, and drank a bottle of water.

The pain quickly subsided, so I started down the hallway again to the meeting. My presentation was successful, so that evening, I met a couple of business associates for dinner to celebrate. At bedtime that night, I thought about the chest-pain I had earlier. It could not be dire, because I exercise and eat healthy foods, I thought. I convinced myself to forget about it.

I had never missed a deadline at work before, but we were working with a challenging new client. Nothing seemed to please them. Usually, commercials with happy families, babies, or children playing with puppies satisfied our clients. If they were trying to appeal to an adult audience, we used attractive scantily dressed supermodels. I didn't know how to solve the problem. I worked late nights on revisions, skipped dinner a few nights, and was having difficulty sleeping. I had given them a plethora of commercials to choose from; however, they rejected all of them. Our deadline was rapidly approaching.

I awoke later than usual in the morning prepared to present the final pitch of another commercial. I had tossed and turned most of the night, so I felt fatigued. I quickly dressed for my appointment with my trainer before work. I grabbed my garment bag and purse, and rushed out of the house.

My gym bag was already in the trunk of my car. As I started the engine, I felt a sharp pain in my chest again. This time my breathing was also labored. I sat very still and sipped water from my bottle. My chest hurt so much that it frightened me. "Dear Lord, please don't let this pain be a heart attack!"

I began to recite a prayer that Nana taught me when I was a child. Once I calmed down, and the pain had subsided, I drove myself to the emergency room. I was given a thorough examination at the hospital. Following a long wait, the doctor informed me that I had not suffered a heart attack. Instead, I had a panic attack.

"Ms. Walton, Have you been experiencing any stress?" The doctor questioned.

"Of course, I am under stress. Who isn't?" I said too loudly.

The doctor recommended that I contact a therapist as soon as possible. He gave me a shortlist of the names of psychologists.

Later that day, after our final presentation, thankfully, our most challenging clients were satisfied. I felt like I could breathe again. I pulled out the list I was given at the hospital and began to search for one of the psychologists on the internet. After reading information about each one on the list, I decided to call Dr. Cora Banks for an appointment the following week.

The next week, I found myself in the office of a pleasant, middle-aged psychologist, Dr. Cora Banks, Ph.D. She had a warm smile and a very soothing voice. She questioned: "Ms. Walton, what brings you here to see me today?" All the while was looking attentively into my eyes.

"I had severe chest pains, so believing I was having a heart attack and ended up in the emergency room. After an examination, I found out that I had a panic attack. I am having trouble getting to sleep at night, so I have been exhausted. The attending physician prescribed a mild anti-anxiety medication. He handed me a list of psychologists and suggested that I make an appointment with one of them. After much research, you are the one I chose."

"Okay. Do you mind describing your parents?" Dr. Banks asked.

"Yes, I can do that," was my response. I pulled my thoughts together and began.

"My mother died when I was a baby. My grandmother, Nana, moved in with us, to help him raise me after my mother passed away.

My father owns his own business and works all the time. He is what most people would call a self-made man. He is quite successful.

When I was younger, during early morning jogs together in the park, my father taught me many things about the world. I enjoyed those beautiful sunny mornings with him. I believe those were the best times we ever had.

As a child, I never understood why he always had a sad look on his face. As an adult, I realize he must have missed my mother. He was not prepared to raise a kid." I continued.

"My grandmother didn't ask Daddy to do very much, but she demanded that he show up for all my birthday parties, with a large cake. Of course, she always handled everything else. It was the least he could do, but he usually showed up late and begrudgingly brought the cake to the table. I guess he loved me, but I am not sure.

"You are not sure if he loves you?" Dr. Banks questioned.

He doesn't care about anyone. I am not sure if he even loves himself. One of the reasons why he was bitter, is because my grandfather abandoned him and Nana when he was twelve years old. My granddad ran off with his secretary and died soon after. He had a massive coronary. My dad refused to attend the funeral. My grandmother, along with her sister, Aunt Mary, did attend.

Nana had been a devoted housewife and mother. She had never worked outside the house. When his father left them, she had to find a job. My grandfather paid for the house they lived in and my father's education, but my grandmother had to pay for everything else.

Since my grandfather didn't have any other children; he never bothered to change his will. Nana inherited everything when he died. She even owned the house that he had shared with his mistress. "The mistress got her just deserts." Nana often said. I guess that meant his secretary got what she deserved!

After checking over her notes, Dr. Banks looked up and said, "Okay, Ms.

Walton, it's time for us to end our session for today. Let us stop here and continue at our therapy session next week. I look forward to hearing more about you and your family."

"Thank you very much, Dr. Banks. I will check my schedule and call to make an appointment. By the way, you can call me Jazzy."

NINE

During our next session, I began. "My Nana is a social butterfly who loves entertaining family and friends. We had a screened-in back porch with beautiful white rocking chairs. She often invited her guests to come over and enjoy time eating, relaxing, and gossiping on our back porch. She had many friends, so it seemed that they were always visiting.

Her friends trusted and respected Nana. They often confided in her. Nobody could keep a secret better than her. Sometime, she would loan people money. She would fold up dollars and wrap them up in a handkerchief and quietly place it in their hand.

Whenever her friends were not around, Nana and I spent time together. I loved the sound of her laughter. I believe that if I became blind, I would recognize her laugher anywhere.

Most days, I would sit on a large pillow at her feet, while she gently brushed my hair, softly singing gospel songs to me. She has a lovely voice and sang in our church choir. After that, she would fold our laundry while I played with my Barbie dolls on our back porch.

The weather in southern Louisiana, where I grew up, is usually warm for most of the year. Our back yard had lots of tall trees that provided lots of shade.

Whenever her friends came over for a visit, I was sent to the backyard to play.

Nana would say: "Baby, fresh air, and exercise are good for you, so go outside and play, but don't leave the backyard."

"Okay, Nana," I would say. I had lots of room to play outside because our yard was vast and beautiful. Nana had a lovely colorful flower garden. We also had a large vegetable garden. We had several fruit trees in a back yard along with a pecan grove."

Dr. Banks allowed me to continue speaking without interruption. I continued.

"I would find a spot very close to our porch, so I could hear the adults were talking. Listening to Nana and her friends was much more interesting than anything my friends had to say. I found most of their conversations fascinating and funny.

She had a way of making anyone feel better. Most people left our house with a smile on their faces, no matter how grim the circumstances. The majority of women who came to see her wanted to gossip or to borrow money from Nana. Some of the things they talked about were difficult for me to comprehend.

Once, I heard her friend Ms. Sally say, "Carol should have rubbed some of that cream on her belly every night as he told her. If she had listened to me, her stomach would not resemble the outside of a ripe fig. You know that daughter of mine never listens to a word I say. She could have easily prevented those stretch marks on her stomach."

We have two large fig trees in our yard. Nana and I picked up the figs soon after they fell to the ground. They tasted sweet, and

Nana used them to make preserves. I walked over and picked one fig off the tree. Then I inspected it thoroughly and popped it into my mouth.

Carol would have those marks on her stomach for the rest of her life, so I decided right then and there that I did not want one of those babies to make my stomach look like that fig. How did that baby get there anyway? I wondered for a second. The story was disturbing, but then my friend from next door came over to our yard to play. I quickly forgot all about her stomach. I started to reflect on my memory. Then I shared more of my life story with Dr. Banks. Another day, I overheard our neighbor, Mrs. Smith, say to Nana, "That darn fool should have known better, everybody knows Shirley has a knife, and she knows how to use it!

Then she said, I heard she tried to cut off his balls, but his friends convinced her to stop. I wondered where Mr. Jones balls were attached to his body, and why Ms. Shirley wanted to cut them off. I just figured that he must be hiding them inside his clothes somewhere.

Ms. Shirley did cut him somewhere on his body because the ambulance came to take him to the hospital. They were mean to laugh about what happened to Mr. Jones.

I was happy that she did not take any of his balls away. He might need them to play again when he got out of the hospital. I laughed during our session as I remembered my thought back then about Mr. Jones.

Life with Nana was never dull. I am sure I learned things that a child should not have been aware of, but it was fun growing up with my grandmother at our house. For the most part, she tried very hard to make my childhood as pleasant and safe as possible. I loved her, but I wanted to spend more time with my dad. I also longed for my mother."

After answering several thought-provoking questions, during our therapy sessions, Dr. Banks made an interesting observation.

I listened to her suggestion intently, then responded. "It sounds like you believe I have unfinished business from my youth. You think I need to make some changes in my life. Where should I begin?"

"It seems to me, that the best place to start is at the beginning," she interjected.

"Start at the beginning? I repeated and stared at her in confusion. Are you suggesting I should start back home, in Louisiana?"

"Jazzy, can you think of a better place to start?" she asked. You will have to take baby steps. I believe all the answers are there for you to uncover."

I was ready for changes in my life so I could relieve my stress. However, I was not quite prepared to look for answers at home, so I decided to try other things.

"I will give that idea a lot of thought," I replied.

"Okay Jazzy, It is time for this session to come to an end."

TEN

After a few sessions with Dr. Banks, my life started to change in small ways. Since she suggested I should start with small step, I purchased a large plant for my living room. I also bought two beautiful paintings of landscapes. One of them reminded of the beaches on a Caribbean Island. I filled the kitchen cabinets with china, glasses, pots, and pans. I began to turn my small house into a home.

I listened to music and danced around my kitchen while preparing dinner a few times each week. I had picked up a few cooking lessons from Nana. Her food was always quite tasty. I was slowly beginning to enjoy my own company, and a glass of red wine with my meal didn't hurt either.

I was not ready to work on any unfinished business back home yet. Instead, I planned a long Labor Day weekend trip, to an island in Mexico, all by myself. The idea was daunting at first, but I believed that I was strong enough for the task at hand. Nervously, I made reservations at a resort where I had stayed a couple of times before with friends. I loved the resort and believed I would be safe there alone.

It was my first trip since my panic attack. Dr. Banks had recommended small steps. Little did she know that this trip was a giant leap? The flight to Mexico went smoothly. The first-class flight attendants were friendly and extremely accommodating. I observed that they seemed to linger and smile a little more with the male passengers.

Soon after reading a few chapters in the latest best-seller and watching a movie, the pilot announced that we should fasten our seatbelts. He was beginning the descent onto the small Mexican island. He was a great pilot because I barely felt a bump when the airplane touched the ground.

"This is a tiny airport in comparison to the one in Atlanta." I said to myself as I looked out the window of the aircraft.

Going through customs was a breeze. It was a little overwhelming passing through the maze of smiling faces trying to sign me up for free tickets to everything worth seeing on the island. Nothing is free in life, so the real price to pay was ninety minutes of your precious time in a timeshare presentation, and that was not for me.

As I maneuvered through the sea of salespeople, I finally recognized my name, J. Walton, on one of the signs held by a driver sent from the resort where I had made reservations. He was tall with a friendly smile. After he greeted me and introduced himself, he retrieved my luggage.

"Ms. Walton, will you please follow me? The car is in front of the airport. The resort is only ten minutes away, and we should be there quickly." Then Victor held open the back door as I slid onto the soft leather back seat of the white limousine. I began to relax as I inhaled the glorious salt sea air.

Upon entering the resort, I quickly found the registration desk and checked in, and then I was escorted to my suite. It was luxurious with a perfect view of the ocean. After handing the young bellman a generous tip, he assured me that if I needed anything during my stay, I could ask for him at the bell stand. His name was Jamie.

"Gracious Jamie, I will remember to call if I need anything. How long does the main restaurant stay open in the evening?"

"It will close at ten, but tonight we will have live entertainment and lots of food at the pool party. You will have lots of fun, Ms. Walton, I am certain."

"I will keep the party in mind."

"In the meantime, we have room service at any time if you are hungry," Jamie said.

"Good to know, but I had lunch on the plane." I thanked him again. Then, I closed the door.

After the bellman left, I unpacked my bag and hung my outfits in the large closet. I took a bottle of water from the refrigerator and went out of the French doors to the balcony. I reclined on a comfortable chair and started reading the novel I brought for the trip.

I guess I was more tired than I thought because I fell asleep on the large comfortable patio chair on the balcony. I awoke to the sound of live music somewhere below. Well rested, after a lovely two-hour nap, I jumped into the shower and changed into a silky floral print dress. I brushed my hair, applied a little make-up, and headed downstairs to the pool party.

Jamie was correct about the party. The live band was very entertaining, and the food smelled great. Famished, I ordered the grilled seafood and the resort drink of the day. The food was spicy and tasty. Several couples were on the small dance floor, moving to the beat of the band. They were having fun; after all, we were here on vacation.

After I finished my dinner, I decided to take a walk on the beach. The sun was setting, and the colors it provided over the water were gorgeous. I felt safe because the resort had security everywhere. The officers were wearing white linen tunics and pants. I wondered if they were wearing holsters with guns. It didn't matter anyway because they were large and looked intimidating.

Walking along the shoreline, I saw several couples walking on the beach also. They seemed so comfortable and content. I felt the breeze from the ocean flowing through my hair. I went back to my suite and reclined on the balcony again until the music stopped. Then I went to bed. The first day of my vacation had been a perfect.

ELEVEN

Very early the next morning, Arden called to ask my opinion about a campaign he was working on with one of our oldest clients. His company had been with our agency since its inception. Since Arden was in the office on Labor Day weekend. I knew the call had to be urgent!

"How are you enjoying your greatly needed vacation, Jazzy?"

"Enjoying my own company, can you believe that?" I laughed. "What's wrong, and why are you calling from the office? Do I need to come back today?"

"No, everything is fine here. I only need the answer to a couple of questions about the Johnson Sportswear account. You need to chill, so that panic attack never happens again!"

"I am feeling fine, so don't worry about me. The file you need is titled JSA records. I guess you could not reach my assistant. She went on a Caribbean cruise with her husband."

"No, I couldn't, and this is too important. I am sorry for disturbing you."

"It's not a problem. I was just enjoying my room service breakfast in bed."

"Hope I did not interrupt anything." He laughed.

"I would never tell!" was my response. "You need to hurry up, finish, and get home. I thought you were inviting family over for a cook-out today?"

"We will have it tomorrow. Sorry, you have to miss it, so I will remind Ashley to save you some barbecue."

"Thanks, but I already asked her. I will be home in a couple of days, so hold down the fort until I get back. Be sure and call me again if you have any more questions about the sports account. I will keep my cell close."

After concluding the business call with Arden, I continued to eat my breakfast, then dressed for an early morning run on the beach. The breeze was comfortable, even though the sun shone brightly. Several people were already out enjoying a walk or run along the shoreline. Vendors were setting up their wears, mostly silver jewelry or swimming attire.

I ran three miles, then returned to my suite to shower and change. A walking tour of the small Mexican town was included in my resort reservation package. Dressed and ready to go a couple of hours before the trip began. I decided to visit the Marina less than a block from the resort.

While on my walk, I noticed many shops, restaurants, bars, and businesses. I spotted a small restaurant, and made a plan to return for dinner later that evening. After my short walk around the marina, I returned to the resort and boarded the tour bus.

The first stop on the guided tour was a famous tequila factory, where we learned how the liquor was made. Near the end of our trip, we were given four free shots of the alcohol according to its potency level. After the first shot, I refused the other three.

As an adult, I had learned to appreciate a glass of expensive red wine, but I had never tasted pure tequila before. It was so strong it caused me to tear up after one sip. I watched the other tourist enjoy their free shots. I didn't care much for the taste of the tequila, but I was very impressed with the large agave plants used to make the liquor. They also used it to make agave nectar.

Of course, the tour ended at the gift shop. Everyone was welcome to purchase bottles of tequila, professionally packaged and delivered to any of the resorts or shipped to your home address, or be prepared for the airplane ride to the tourist's next destination. They made it extremely simple for you to buy their products, so I witnessed a lot of sales. I concluded that tourists enjoy drinking tequila.

Our next stop was lunch, it was perfect timing for liquored-up tourists. By then, everyone was friendly and in a good mood. I ordered the fish special, and it was the best I have ever tasted. It had been marinated overnight in some fantastic spices and was served fresh off the grill.

We toured another area called Old Town. It is their downtown area with business offices. It was rustic and beautiful with old-world architecture. We concluded the tour at a beautiful Catholic cathedral, where I said a prayer for my family. I fell asleep on the bus ride back to the resort. It had been a lovely, sunny day. The tour had been enjoyable.

After unloading my shopping bags in my suite, I quickly changed into one of the new bikinis and cover-up, I had purchased while on our tour. I grabbed a beach towel and followed the short trail down to the beach.

I found a great spot and reclined on a lounging beach-chair and ordered one of the sizeable, fruity drink specials of the day. The waiter handed me a sales ticket for me to add my room number and signature. Sipping the delicious cold drink and enjoying the breeze, I took in the impressive view of the aqua blue water.

Time seemed to pass quickly. Before I realized how late it was, the sun began to descend into the ocean. I drifted off to sleep again. When I awoke, it was dinner time. Too tired, hungry, and too tired to walk back to the Marina, I decided to have dinner again at the beach restaurant. The same band was playing live music. They were playing a slow, soothing Latin beat. I enjoyed my dinner as I listened to the music. This time I ordered a decadent dessert.

As the evening progressed, the band started to play dance music. A handsome gentleman, with a hint of grey hair, asked me to dance. The man had an English accent that reminded me of the tall, handsome, famous English actor.

I said, "Yes," and offered him my hand.

"Where is your date tonight? I noticed that you're eating alone," he stated.

"I didn't bring him. Where is your date? You aren't a stalker, are you?" I asked with a knowing smile.

For a second or two, he looked as if searching for the right words to say. He was looking down at first, then finally looked into my eyes and said: "My wife died a couple of years ago, so, unfortunately I am alone. I am not a stalker; actually, I am a financial planner."

"Sorry for your loss, I said. My name is Jazmine."

"Thank you." My name is Matthew.

"Where are you from, Matthew?"

He told me he lived in London. "I am here with my son's wedding party. The rehearsal dinner ended early tonight, but I wasn't ready to go back to my room, so I stopped here to have a drink. The wedding is tomorrow. After hearing the music, I decided to stay awhile. This band is excellent. Do you come to the UK much, Jazmine?"

"No, in the past I traveled a lot for work, but I don't have to anymore."

"Sorry to hear that. I don't frequent the US either. Why did you stop traveling for work? Did you get a big promotion?"

"I guess you could say that," I responded and decided to leave it at that. I wasn't ready to explain that I'm part owner of an advertising agency.

We danced to a couple more songs and talked about our world travels.

"Jazmine, how would you like to crash a small beach wedding tomorrow? I don't have a date. I know I will enjoy your conversation a lot more than my future in-laws. We will have time to get to know each other better. I find you interesting and intriguing."

"Sounds like fun, but I did not pack a dress to wear to a wedding. I would need to buy a new dress. You may be in luck because I was going shopping at the Marina tomorrow anyway. What time is the wedding?"

"It will be at sunset here on this beach. The reception will follow in one of the ballrooms. I think this is the same band scheduled to play at the reception. At least we know the music will be good. So are you saying yes?"

"Yes, I believe I am, if you would accompany me to the Marina in the morning. You can help to pull me away from shopping, so your date won't be late."

"Sure, I would love to accompany you tomorrow. I was planning to go there anyway. I heard that the yachts docked at the marina are beautiful."

"Yes, I agree they are wonderful. I saw a few yachts and large boats in port yesterday morning."

"Let's meet tomorrow morning in the lobby at 9:00 a.m. I think I will stay here a little longer and enjoy the music. It has been a long time since I felt this alive!" Matthew exclaimed.

"See you in the morning, Matthew. Oh, by the way, my friends call me Jazzy."

TWELVE

I woke up alert and ready for a quick run on the beach. After eating a light breakfast, from the room service menu, I quickly jumped into the shower and prepared for a busy day ahead.

Matthew and I met in the lobby at 9:00 a.m. After a hello embrace, we headed for our shopping trip to the marina. It was another beautiful day. Even though it had rained the night before it did not dampen the beauty of the glorious morning. The sun was glistening brightly on the water at the marina; it was a deep blue color.

I could not wait to tell Nana about my trip to Mexico; she was unaware of it because I didn't want her to worry. It was almost impossible to believe that I found a way to enjoy my first vacation, all by myself. Not completely alone, because I was enjoying the company of a gorgeous Englishman. After a short walk to the marina, we found a small boutique filled with beautiful dresses. Shops were just opening, and sales clerks greeted us with friendly smiles. I looked around for a while. First, I bought a beautiful dress, I knew Nana would love. Then, I continued to search for the perfect dress to wear to the wedding.

"Jazzy, will you be okay while I walk over to the Port Authority Office? It is on the other side of the marina. I'll be back shortly," Matthew said. Later, I discovered that I was not the only one withholding information. Matthew had chartered a yacht for his son and new daughter in-law's honeymoon. He was treating the happy couple to the glorious three-day trip. I didn't find out until he told me later that day at the wedding reception.

Finally, I found a perfect dress for the wedding. When Matthew returned, we headed to the restaurant I spotted the previous morning. We enjoyed a quick lunch. Everything I had eaten, thus far, had been delicious and the food at this restaurant did not disappoint. It was spicy but a different type from the menu in Louisiana.

Ready to get back to my suite, I finished my cup of coffee and asked Matthew if he wanted to return to the Resort. I needed to get back for a massage.

I finished everything a little earlier than I anticipated, so I relaxed on the balcony for a short while. After a brief rest, it was time to get dressed.

Matthew had to be at the wedding early, so I found my way down to the beach, where the chairs were placed for the wedding. I located an excellent place to sit. The weather was perfect for the ceremony, as the sun began to set over the horizon.

He saw me, walked over to where I was sitting, then gave me a quick peck on the cheek. I could tell by the look on his face, he was pleased with the dress I had chosen for this occasion. He had not seen the one I had selected, during the time he was making the final arrangements for the couple's honeymoon.

"Wow, you picked out a winner! You look amazing in that dress. Thank you so much for accepting the invitation to be my date for the wedding."

Shortly after his greeting, the music started. The flower girls and bridesmaids began to walk down the aisle. The groom and best man, along with the minister, were waiting under a beautifully decorated arch with lovely flowers. The view of the beach in the background was so beautiful. I almost cried at the sight of it.

The bride was breathtaking, and the groom looked happy, as his future wife walked down the aisle. Following the wedding, we entered a beautifully decorated ballroom for the reception. The wedding planner had taken care of every detail. There were white tablecloths and tall centerpieces filled with the same fresh tropical flowers as the arch.

Matthews' family was pleased that he found a date for the evening. I enjoyed meeting them. They all spoke with English accents.

The same band, from the beach the night before, was softly playing the music until the bride and groom arrived. After they were seated, the speeches and toast began. When everyone finished, the waiters served us a hot, delicious meal. Most weddings have drab tasting food, but our dinner was delicious fresh seafood and steaks.

The father-daughter dance followed dinner, soon after the dance floor quickly filled with people. The band wasn't playing Latin music today; instead, they were playing the latest, most popular dance songs.

He invited me to join him on the dance floor. He was having a great time, no longer acting like the sad widower, I met earlier. The bride and groom cut the cake, the guest enjoyed it, and then we danced into the night. After the wedding reception ended, he walked me back to my suite. He lingered briefly.

When Matthew told me that, his son and daughter-in-law worked with him in their own financial business, I finally informed him that I was the co-owner of an advertising agency in Atlanta, GA. He did not seem the least bit surprised.

"I would like to thank you, Jazzy, for a wonderful evening. You helped me find my way back to life again, for the first time since I lost my dear wife. I will never forget you. You are invited to my home in London anytime."

In turn, I told him how he helped me enjoy my first solo vacation. He had made my trip more exciting.

Exhausted, I finally said, "I have an early flight back home in the morning, and I need to finish packing." We exchanged numbers and agreed to stay in touch.

"Safe travels, my dear. Good night and sweet dreams." Then he gently kissed me goodbye on my cheek.

"Good night, Matthew, and safe travels to you and your family."

THIRTEEN

Very early, Tuesday morning, I arrived at the small airport an hour early and waited on my flight. I had a great time, however it was time for me to get back to work.

Once, I boarded the airplane, I fell asleep. I slept peacefully on the way back to Atlanta. I had only been gone for four days but it seemed longer. I was happy that my first vacation alone was a great success. I had taken a small step to improve my mental health. I was ready to take the giant leap- a trip back to my hometown.

I was happy to be back, and with a gorgeous tan, I might add. As soon I arrived at my office, I discovered that Matthew had sent me a lovely bouquet of two dozen roses. The card said, "Thank you for reviving me, and hopefully I will see you soon. In the meantime take good care of yourself." I smiled at the memory.

Arden and the rest of my staff welcomed me back. They made inquiries about my trip and the roses too.

The day after I returned from my trip, I made an appointment with Dr. Bank for the following week. I had enjoyed talking with her; I looked forward to our next session.

"Good morning, Dr. Banks."

"Hello Jazzy, how are you today?"

"I haven't had any more chest pains. I am feeling much more relaxed now. I went on a long weekend trip all by myself."

During our session, Dr. Banks asked me to tell her about my trip.

"I enjoyed my weekend in Mexico. I am feeling more secure now. I met a nice man at dinner on the beach the second night. We talked for a long time that night. He invited me to his son's wedding. It was at the resort, and it was a beautiful ceremony on the beach. I had a lot of fun and made some new friends."

Dr. Banks, said, "It sounds like you made progress by taking a trip alone for the very first time. This morning, I would like for you to tell me a little about your past relationships with men. I understand that you are not married. All the men you've mentioned during our sessions, all seem to be friends. Are you romantically involved with anyone? Have you ever been in love?" she inquired.

"My relationships haven't worked out. When I was a teenager I fell in love with a man. One night he told me he was going out of town with his cousin but I saw him in a bar in our hometown talking with some women."

"So you saw him talking to women? "

"Did you ask him why he was there?"

"No. I thought he lied to me so I accused him of cheating."

"Did the two of you ever discuss what happened?"

"No. I didn't want to hear his excuses. I broke up with him and soon after left for college. I never saw him again."

"So how do you know he was cheating if you never talked about what happened? Don't you think he deserves a chance to explain? Everyone needs closure."

"I guess I never thought about that. Looking back now, maybe that was an immature action to take."

"Maybe it is time for you to discover the truth about what happened that night."

"Maybe you are correct, Dr. Banks. It is time for me to find some answers at home."

She assured me that I was ready to go back to Louisiana and face my demons head-on. I agreed and believed that I was confident enough to handle anything I discovered.

"Dr. Banks, my reservations are already confirmed for the journey."

FOURTEEN

As soon as the plane landed in Louisiana, I felt great to be back in the small town where I grew up. It had grown so much, I barely recognized the place. Nana had moved into a townhouse at a senior living community. I was so excited, I could hardly wait to see her. I wanted to apologize for staying away from home for such a long time.

I had to check in at the entrance of her senior community. As soon as I was allowed to enter through the large gates, I quickly discovered that Nana's new home was beautiful. I began to search for Nana, and I found her on the lawn participating in a Tai Chi class. She didn't notice me until her class was finished. As soon as she laid eyes on me, her eyes filled with tears. She quickly walked over and gave me a big hug.

"Hello, my darling Jazmine. I should spank you, young lady, for making me wait so long to see you again."

"Hello Nana, I am happy to see you. I missed you so much!"

I stood there hugging her, and I felt mush love in Nana's arms. For a minute, I was her grandbaby once again. Tears started to roll slowly down my face. I could barely speak. As my grandmother gently wiped tears from my cheeks, I was finally able to say, "Nana, I am so sorry I did not come home sooner."

As she hugged me and expressed kind and endearing words to me, my tears continued to flow. Partly, because I felt guilty for staying away from home so long, but mostly because it felt so amazing to see her again.

"I promise you, I will never stay away again. It was never about you anyway, Nana. You know the real reason why I stayed away so long. How is my father anyway?" I inquired. I did not tell him that I was flying here today."

"Oh, my child, Nana exclaimed, it is time for both of you to heal old wounds and mend those fences. He will be so surprised to see you. He stopped drinking and met someone that cares for him very much. They met almost a year ago at a dinner party and have been spending a lot of time together. She even has him going to church with her on Sundays. Her name is Teresa and she is a retired kindergarten teacher. Your dad is happier than he has been in years. I am sure you will love his friend. She is kind to everyone. I am so happy that you're home, but now it's time for you to go over and have a talk with your father. He is at his office. Why don't you offer to take him to lunch? He will be so surprised to see you, baby. He has a lot he wants to say to you.

I will see you later. I have to go to my yoga class and I don't want to be late. I have to hurry because I want to get a good spot to lay down my yoga mat. Tonight I am preparing all your favorite foods for dinner, plus, your Nana is making you a peach cobbler. Be sure to invite your dad and remind him to bring his girlfriend, Teresa, also. We will eat around 7:00 p.m.

By the way Jazmine, please be patient with your father. He has been trying very hard to turn his life around."

"I love you Nana and I am looking forward to the best dinner in town tonight."

I left for my father's office and parked my rental car close to his office building. I said a small prayer before entering the building.

"Hello. My name is Jazmine Walton. I am here to see my father. Will you let him know I'm here, please?"

"Good morning, Ms. Walton, I am sorry but he is in a meeting. They should be finished in a few minutes. Will you have a seat? As soon as they are finished, I will let him know you are here."

"Thank you, he isn't expecting me so I don't mind waiting until his meeting is over."

"As you wish, Ms. Walton," she said.

"You can call me Jazzy."

"Okay, Jazzy. Would you like something to drink, perhaps a bottle of water?"

"No thank you. I'll just sit here and wait."

Sitting there, I thought about how my father never spoke of my mother. It seemed to cause him too much pain. I believed that was the reason he was sad. I learned to stop asking him any questions about her. I only had an old picture of her that Nana gave me when I was a child, and I kept it in my wallet.

After a few minutes, my father walked out of his office with a couple of gentlemen. He saw me sitting there and a broad smile formed on his face. I didn't even know he had teeth because I don't ever remember seeing him smile. He was always sad or grumpy. I don't ever remember seeing my father happy.

Daddy's eyes shone brightly as he proudly announced to his clients, "This is my lovely daughter Jazmine." Then he walked over and hugged me. I just stood there shocked.

As Nana requested, Dad and I had a long lunch and he said many things that needed to be said.

"I know I was never present for you and I regret that very much. I relied too much on my mother to provide the love I should have given you myself. I am sorry for that. I will try my best to make it up to you. I realize how much precious time I have wasted. I love you so much, my darling child, I hope you will forgive me."

Later that night, Daddy brought his friend, Teresa, to Nana's for dinner. She was very pleasant and I enjoyed talking with her.

"He has a good tenor voice, so I am trying to convince him to join the church choir," said Teresa.

"That would be a sight to see." I thought as I glanced over at Nana. We were both trying very hard not to laugh. I liked Teresa. I was pleased that my father and Nana had found new lives and were happy.

Nana always liked to tell one of her favorite stories about me. She told Teresa that when I was a small child, l would place my toys on the floor in front of the television to play. Whenever a commercial started, I would stop and intensely stare at the television, and if there was music playing during the commercial, I would dance along with the tune. "I suppose, Jazmine's advertising career began with a love for commercials at a very early age," Nana remarked.

FIFTHTEEN

The following morning, I woke up late from a dream or was it a nightmare? I was covered with sweat. It felt so real and I could clearly see his smiling face. I had not thought about him in years. I assumed the memories were flowing because I was back home again.

In my dream, he was asking me a question, "What did you tell your grandmother before you left the house?" I clearly remembered that first night because it was the most amazing time of my life. That was the night I became a woman. It was equally frightening and exciting.

Paul could sense my anxiety and asked me, "Jazzy are you sure about this?" He was making sure that I understood what I was agreeing to do. Our plan was to spend the night together in New Orleans. The city was about an hour's drive from our small hometown. It was my favorite city in the world. Nana had given me permission to spend the night at Diane's house. She was having a pool party and all of our senior class was invited. I drove her car to Diane's but only stayed there for a short time. I felt guilty because I had never lied to my grandmother before. Instead of spending the night at Diane's house, Paul and I went to a jazz festival in the city. Afterward, we went on a tour of the beautiful city and then checked into a luxurious five-star hotel.

We rested for a while, then dressed for a romantic candlelight dinner at a nearby restaurant. After dinner, we went for a walk along the riverfront. It was a warm summer night, and tourists were also out for a stroll. We held hands and enjoyed the moonlight and the stars.

He whispered sweet things into my ear. "Jazzy, you look radiantly beautiful tonight. I love your new dress; that color looks wonderful next to your glowing skin. Looks like you got a tan at the festival today.

How will you explain it to Nana when you get back home tomorrow?"

"I hate lying to Nana here. Even if she notices, I'm sure she'll think I was lounging out by the swimming pool with my friends. Anyway, you seem to be the only one that recognizes any small changes in my face."

"That's because you always look so lovely, my dear and you always smell great too. Are you wearing a new perfume tonight? That scent is almost hypnotic. I've never smelled that fragrance before."

"Yes, it's new. Nana just bought it for me. She said I should smell more like a mature adult since I'm going off to college."

He looked a little sad when I mentioned going away to college. He tried to hide it with a smile and jokes, but his eyes were not as bright and joyful. I could tell because I knew most of the expressions on his face. I guess I studied him the same way he studied me. We walked slowly back to the hotel where he had rented a suite for us, with a view of the river. He could tell I was nervous, so he suggested that maybe we should take a hot shower.

"Together?" I asked a bit louder than I had expected it to sound! He had seen me in my bikini many times before, but I had never been exposed in front of a man.

He stripped away all of his clothes. Then slowly and lovingly began to peel my clothes away. He started singing softly because I think he thought it would help me to relax. I timidly joined him in the shower. He continued to sing softly as he used a soapy sponge to wash my back. He kissed me on the back of my neck and gently turned me around to face him.

He used a large towel to dry my cold body. I was trembling. He gently lifted me off the floor and carried me to the large king-size bed.

"Jazmine are you awake?" Nana was calling my name. "Come downstairs now and eat breakfast before your father leaves for work."

Wow that was a hell of a dream. I had not thought about him for a very long time. Memories of Paul were intruding my sleep. I began to wonder about him once again. He had always been a kind gentleman, most often encouraging to others. It had been impossible to find another man to fill his shoes. I had used that as an excuse to never fully give my heart to another. I was afraid of getting hurt again. Even though he continued to live in the same small town where I grew up, I never ran into him during my visits to see Nana and my father. I was always in a rush to get back to work at the advertising agency.

Little did I know, I was about to run into him that very day right in front of Nana's favorite dress shop. After ten years the inevitable happened.

SIXTEEN

Since I was already back home, Nana asked: "While you are here visiting are you planning to attend your tenth high school's class reunion? It would be nice for you to see some of your old classmates. They are always asking me about you, especially your old friend Diane. Isn't she the one that use to drive you around in her father's dilapidated old car?

She is married now with a couple of kids. You and your friends used to spend a lot of time having fun together before you left for college. She told me that she hasn't seen you in years. She doesn't understand why you have been so distant and she feels that she has done or said something to upset you."

"The last time I saw my friend Dianne was that awful Saturday night we went looking for her cheating boyfriend, who later became her husband and father of her children. I guess he finally grew up."

"You are so much like your father in that respect. You just can't walk away from your friends or enemies without communicating. Neither one of you can have closure because you bury your feelings then run away and hide. Both of you should learn a way to resolve your problems the same way you do in the business world!"

"I know you're right, Nana. Dr. Banks agrees with you. The closure is extremely important for your health and well-being."

"Who is Dr. Banks?" Nana asked.

"She's my new physician," I answered. However, I didn't tell Nana what kind of doctor. I wasn't ready to admit I was in therapy.

To change the subject, I exclaimed, "I was invited to my high school reunion by e-mail. However, I have been so busy. Since I didn't respond, it may be too late."

"You were too busy to attend your first class reunion. Most of your friends have not seen you in almost a decade. You look practically the same, but your body has filled out in all the best places," Nana laughed, "I am sure they will recognize their old captain of the football cheerleading squad as soon as you walk into that gymnasium. Let's go shopping tomorrow for the perfect party dress," Nana said excitedly!

"I would love to go with you to Sally's Dress Shop on Main Street. I had planned to buy a couple of party dresses there anyway. I love the way she alters her dresses. They are tailored to fit perfectly.

Good night, Nana. I am going to bed now. It has been a very long day and I am pretty tired. I will be ready to go shopping after breakfast in the morning."

"Okay Honey. Since you are going to be home for the whole week, don't forget to respond to the email about the reunion dance."

The following day after breakfast, we went shopping for a dress to wear to my class reunion and I saw him. Paul looked the same as he had in my dream the previous night. He had not aged at all. He was still the beautiful man I had fallen in love with a long time ago.

He was walking down the sidewalk holding onto the hand of a very pretty little girl. She was looking up at him chatting and smiling as she held onto a large red balloon. There was an attractive, petite young woman on the other side of the little girl. He did not see me or Nana as they walked past us, and thankfully Nana did not see him either.

The next night, I attended my class reunion. It was great to see my high school friends again. I was especially overjoyed to see my old friend Diane. To my surprise, she was married to the man we were searching for that Saturday night ten years ago. I guess he wasn't cheating after all.

They had been married at the courthouse eight years ago and have a seven-year-old son. She is a media specialist at our old high school. Her husband Peter was kind and attentive to Diane. She showed me pictures of their son, which she was very proud of. I invited them to come to Atlanta for a visit at any time. We exchanged numbers and promised to stay in touch.

I reacquainted myself with my former cheerleading squad, and debate team members. I felt guilty because I had not stayed in touch with any of my old high school friends. Several of them were married with children and continued to live in Louisiana. That night, I danced and laughed and looked at several pictures of my friends' children on their cell phones.

I had a wonderful evening. I vowed that if it was possible, I would attend more of our class reunions in the future. For a long time, I had separated myself from the people I loved growing up. It was time for that to come to an end. When our reunion dance came to an end, several of us hugged goodbye and a few tears were shed. We posed together for several pictures and agreed to reach out more in the future.

After returning to my hometown, life seemed a little sweeter. I finally had a chance to enjoy Nana's companionship from a woman's perspective. We loved sharing information, shopping, and talking about life in general.

My father had changed so much. I guess you could say the love of a good woman helped, but I believe it was because he found a way to overcome his past. He found joy in his life again.

On Sunday afternoon, I flew back to Atlanta. It had been a wonderful trip. I promised Nana and Daddy that I would return soon. I thought about Paul and his new woman and child on my flight home. I finally felt free of a burden I had been carrying around for a very long time! I realized it was time to move on with my life. I had a lot to tell Dr. Banks at our final session.

SEVENTEEN

One very cold winter morning, in my Atlanta office, I was unconsciously pacing back and forth. I was dealing with a difficult new client and none of our commercials pleased him. I was having difficulty concentrating. For us, the dilemma was to come up with a new concept for a new line of women's clothing. As I paced, I happened to glance out my office window, which was on the 12th floor of a high rise building on Peachtree Street. I noticed several police cars lined up in front of our office building. I also saw the large S.W.A.T. truck parked on the sidewalk at the entrance of the building. I didn't know what all the commotion was about, so I stepped outside my office door into the hallway in order to find out. As I stepped out of my office, I looked to my right and a man with a gun in his hand popped out of the stairwell door. I stood, frozen in my tracks, as he covered my mouth with his large hand before I could scream. He grabbed me and shoved me back into my office. I didn't know what was happening. He locked the door and told me to get down.

"I will shoot you if you make a sound." He began to pace the floor and started to mumble something to himself. As he moved around my office with the gun, he never pointed it directly at me. Instead he pointed it at the door the entire time, as though expecting someone to burst through it at any minute. I was terribly afraid. I believed that this may be the last day of my life. All I could think about was Nana's lovely face. I knew she would want me to be brave. I thought about how much pain my father and I caused each other. I vowed that I would forgive him if I ever had another chance.

All of a sudden, I heard noise and activity outside my office. I couldn't see anything because the man had closed the blinds to the windows. I learned later that the

S.W.A.T. team was moving our staff out of the offices of the agency.

My office telephone started to ring. I nearly jumped out of my skin. I did not move and he did not move either. He stopped pacing and mumbling. The phone continued to ring, but I refused to answer. I didn't move an inch.

Finally, he yelled, "Answer that damn thing!"

I quickly grabbed the phone and put it on the speaker. "Hello, this is J and A Advertising Agency."

"Is this Ms. Jazmine Walton?" the man asked.

"Yes this is Jazmine,'" was my timid response.

"This is Officer Smith. Will you put Mr. Johnson on speaker phone please?" He asked quickly.

"He is listening."

Mr. Johnson grabbed the telephone receiver, and simply and calmly stated: "I want a clear exit out of this building, or I am going to kill this young lady. I have nothing left to lose. They have stolen everything from me. Call me back when you develop a plan."

Then he turned to me, "Those people in the financial offices, on the 10th floor, stole all of our money! They took everything away from me all of my children's college funds and all my retirement savings. My wife is battling breast cancer they stole her life from me! That is the reason why I shot that Son of a Bitch, in the office downstairs. I am so sorry that I have to hold you, hostage, in here, but as you heard me say, if the cops don't provide a way for me to leave this building, I will kill you and myself."

I remained quiet and very still, as I stayed seated on the floor. I didn't want to upset this deranged man. Obviously, he had killed someone already and was willing to kill me and himself also. He began to pace again, back and forth. His pacing was making me nervous. I made a vow to never pace again if by God's grace I lived to see another day. He reminded me of a caged animal. I could see the sweat on his brow and the fear in his eyes, as he moved around my office.

Then all of a sudden he asked, "Do you have any water in here?"

"Yes, I do. There are bottles in the bottom drawer of my desk. Over there," I said and pointed.

He allowed me to get up from the floor to get him a bottle of water. There was a small revolver in my purse in that same desk drawer. I thought: "If he allows me to get the water, I may have been able to get to my revolver. He was a quick thinker, and he walked over to the desk with me. He opened the bottom drawer for himself and pulled out a couple of bottles of water. He handed me one.

I guess Mr. Johnson got tired of pacing, because he sat down in one of my office chairs. The phone began to ring again. Just as he reached the phone, on my desk, the shot rang out! The office was soundproof, so Mr. Johnson did not hear the helicopter as it hovered. A sniper shot him. I screamed and screamed, as I watched him fall to the floor of my office.

EIGHTEEN

Waking up in a hospital bed, I was disoriented. Nana was holding my hand with tears rolling down her face. I thought I was waking up from a dream until I felt the pain.

As the man holding me hostage, fell to the floor he accidently discharged his automatic weapon and the bullet grazed my left shoulder. I was waking up from emergency surgery in Emory Hospital. Daddy was out in the corridor, as he was handling business on his cell phone.

"Hey Nana, don't cry. What are you doing here?" I asked.

"Do you remember what happened Jazmine?" All my life Nana had always called me by my given name. However, this time, as she spoke my name, I could see pain and worry in her eyes. "Baby, you were wounded, with a gun, by a mad man, but he is dead now."

"Oh, Nana, I cried, I remember watching as a sniper shot him. He accidentally shot me as he fell to the floor. He was a very troubled and a sad man. He was angry about his investment with the company on the tenth floor. He came up the stairwell as I stepped out of my office and grabbed me before I knew what was happening. I guess I was at the wrong place at the wrong time. He grabbed me and forced me into my office before I could warn everyone to get out."

"The police officers got them out safely. Baby, there was nothing you could have done to help them. I am so happy you are alive and well."

My father walked into the room and gave me a gentle hug. "As soon as your doctor discharges you and you can fly, we are taking you home to Louisiana so Nana can nurse you back to health. I have chartered a private jet. There will be no arguments from you, young lady."

The last thing I wanted to do was argue. That was one of the best ideas he ever had, I thought as I drifted back to sleep.

I stayed with Nana and Daddy for a few weeks to recuperate. During my visit, I was able to mend some broken relationships. I returned to my office in Atlanta well mended, both in heart and soul. It was great to be back at work again.

NINETEEN

Nana died peacefully in her sleep at the nursing home in Louisiana, where she lived for the last year of her life. I was not there, but in my heart I believe she passed away with a lovely smile on her face. I had spent time with her during the Christmas season, a few weeks before she passed away. The holiday had been her most joyous time of every year.

I went home to help my father plan her funeral. I did not feel nearly as sad as I thought I would. Her home-going was beautiful, but Daddy seemed overwhelmed with grief. He had lost the one woman that stood by him no matter what, from the time he was born until the day she died. They were very close. I knew he would miss her very much.

I knew where her soul was resting, because she had prepared me for this day. She was in the arms of our Lord, and had talked about it in great detail during my last visit. Nana made it sound as if she was taking a trip to a wonderful place and did not want us to be sad.

Daddy and I went to dinner, at a local family restaurant, soon after Nana's funeral. We ran into many of our family friends. They expressed their condolences. Nana was very well known in our small town and she had touched so many lives. It brought a smile to my face to hear so many wonderful, heartfelt stories about her. They laughed and told jokes. I laughed so hard I cried.

Nana had lived in our small home town all her life. She didn't care much for traveling, and reserved that for emergencies. She drove a black Lincoln, but never so far away from home. Sometimes, she would shop in New Orleans, but only for special occasions. We would take the train into the city. Since she did the majority of her shopping locally, she had contributed a great deal of money to the town's economy. The business owners knew her by name.

Generally, she never drove her Lincoln too far from home. Since we never visited many other places, when I was old enough to travel, I visited many places around the world.

After I dried my eyes, I glanced out of the front window of the restaurant and could not believe my eyes. Paul was standing on the sidewalk with his broad shoulders, tanned skin, and pearly white teeth. He had a short well-groomed beard, but other than that his appearance had not changed in a decade.

At first he didn't see me, so I was able to watch him for a short time from my chair in the window. He was helping an elderly gentleman load some heavy items into the back of his truck. Afterward, he shook the gentleman's hand and smiled. The old man's grandson got out of the truck and gave Paul a hug. As he waved goodbye to them, he headed back to the sidewalk.

He glanced into the window of the restaurant and stood for a minute in that spot. At first, he looked a little baffled. Then after a few seconds he started to smile. He moved slowly toward the window as I stood there for a moment unable to move. Finally, I pressed my hands on the window as he did the same thing on the other side. We stood there frozen in time. Then he pointed toward the door and we both quickly started in that direction.

I heard my father say, "Go to him Jazzy. He has been waiting for you so long" Shockingly, Daddy had granted a large contract to Paul's construction company, not realizing, beforehand, who he was. I wondered why my father kept it a secret from me until now. "Give him a second chance. He deserves it and so do you."

"Thanks, Daddy, I will!" I said as my feet began to gain momentum, rushing toward the door.

By the time I stepped outside, the love of my life was waiting with his arms opened wide and I ran straight into them. He kissed me and it took my breath away. I could hear a familiar song in my heart, one that I had not heard in a very long time. With the pad of his thumbs he wiped away the tears from my eyes. His touch felt as though electricity was coursing through on my body. The touch I remembered from our past. It was the familiar touch that I had never felt with anyone else. He lifted my chin, pressed his lips against mine, and then gave me the gentlest kiss. I looked up at him and smiled back. Then I wrapped my arms around his neck and kissed him with the passion I felt for him for as long as I could remember. He felt like home. I felt so silly, after he explained that the woman and child I saw with him was his cousin and her child. Also he and my father had been working together on several contracts. Daddy had grown to like and respect him.

Finally, after several long years, I gave him a chance to explain why he was in that bar with his cousin and not in New Orleans. He told me that he took him there to see his children and his wife refused. His drinking was the reason she left him in the first place.

"I knew he had a serious problem. I was afraid to leave him alone because he was so depressed. He asked me to stop at the bar for one last drink and foolishly I agreed. When I went to the restroom, he took the keys off the bar and put them in his pocket. He worked with the women you saw that night, but I did not know them. I couldn't leave him there because he was too drunk to drive."

Then Paul told me that he had never returned to New Orleans after that night. He leaned in very close to my ear and whispered, "How would you like to go there tomorrow night for dinner, Jazzy?"

I could barely contain the joy I felt at that moment. My heart was beating so fast, it felt as though it was going to jump out of my chest. I began to cry tears of joy and he lightly kissed them away. Then we embraced and kissed fervently as time stood still.

"Yes, I would love to go back there again with you! I have never been back there, either. After all, it is my favorite city." This was the perfect time for both of us. Our paths had crossed again and led us to right here, right now. We were back in each other's arms, with no regrets.

"My God, Jazzy, what took you so long?" He asked, as he held me tightly in his arms. "It was worth the wait."

TWENTY

One year later, we were married in Nana's lovely garden in early spring. All her flowers were in bloom. Somehow, I know she would be pleased with me. Visualizing her smiling down from heaven; I could feel her spirit very near. I smiled as my father walked me down the aisle to my handsome future husband. My heart began to flutter at the first sign of him standing at the altar waiting patiently.

Daddy had invited all of our friends and neighbors to the wedding. Our reception was a wonderful feast of Nana's old Cajun recipes, and we also served lots of wine and champagne. The party lasted long into the night, and everyone seemed to have a wonderful time. I had never seen my father as happy as he was on our wedding day.

Paul and I left the reception around midnight, for a honeymoon in Paris. My father had his private jet, a Gulfstream, ready for our departure. It was his wedding present to us. We were very excited and looking forward to a couple of weeks, in France.

We had built a new home in Texas, and planned to move into it after we returned from our honeymoon. It was a huge ranch style house with a large outdoor living area and a swimming pool. It sits in the middle of five acres of land. We built it in Texas, very close to the Louisiana state line.

We wanted to live close enough to commute to our businesses. We needed to live in a location, where we could both continue our careers.

Paul had several construction contracts with my father's commercial real estate company, so he would continue to manage his construction business.

Arden and I opened our second advertising agency, in a small town near Houston. He and his wife Ashley wanted to continue to live in Atlanta. Arden would become president of our Georgia agency, and I would manage the new firm in Texas.

Some of our staff would move from Georgia and join me in Houston. Some of them had left the Dallas firm to work for us in Atlanta. They were happy to move closer to their extended families in Texas.

Arden and I agreed that our advertising agencies would be more productive if I handled our clients in the western half the US. And he would handle the ones in the east. I wanted everything taken care of before we left for Paris.

Our flight was flawless. We had dinner on the plane, and afterward, slept until our arrival in Europe. For our honeymoon, we checked into The Hotel Ambassador. It had great staff, friendly, kind, and accommodating people. There were several cafes along the sidewalks nearby. Most of the tourist attractions were within walking distance of our hotel also.

One of the concierges recommended a rooftop restaurant close by, and we walked there in the moonlight. He said that it had a perfect view of Paris. After we arrived and were seated, we looked around. The view was amazing. I thought: "Paris is the most romantic city in the world. After dinner, we enjoyed watching the "Eiffel Tower" from the balcony of our suite. The lights shone brightly from the tower every night. It was indeed a magnificent sight to behold. It had been a wise decision to share my first trip to Paris with my husband.

On our second day, we went on tours of the "Eiffel Tower" and "Notre Dame Cathedral," where we said silent prayers. That night we had tickets to a show at the "Mulan Rouge." The following day, we went on a boat ride along the Siege River. It was like a taxi on the water.

The first stop was the "Louvre Museum." We wanted to see that picture the painting of the Mona Lisa and a statue of David. We saw paintings of The Madonna and Jesus. There were so many beautiful pieces of art; it would take days to see all of them. We were there for the majority of the day.

For dinner, we ate at a restaurant called "Au Petite Riche," where we dined on seafood. Our appetizer was a crepe filled with a cheese sauce and crab meat, and for the entrée, we shared seafood pasta dish. Paul also ordered grilled fish. I also had my first glass of Lambrusco. Our meal was fantastic.

We shared a view of the "Arch de Triumphs," from the back of a taxi, after the sunset. There are several bridges in Paris, and that evening we walked across a bridge with many locks attached. It was a tradition for lovers to leave them there, so we purchased two small locks at a shop nearby and added them to the collection.

While we were there on our honeymoon, we walked almost everywhere we went. Paul enjoyed being outdoors. He seemed to view the city in wonderment, as though seeing it through the eyes of a child.

I loved his eyes; they were warm, caring, and always filled with joy. I saw him in a different light, as I watched him that night. I could see his feelings, because he wore it on his sleeve, but I could still see his glorious chiseled face, muscular body, and glowing bronze skin. It was kissed by the sun from several years working outside. The look of the man I loved made me feel warm and tingly.

The following morning we got up early and went on a shopping trip on the "Champs Elyse". The prices at the stores were very reasonable. I bought clothes, shoes, and jewelry. Paul only purchased a watch. He didn't care much for shopping, but he did care a great deal about whatever gave his wife pleasure.

We had skipped breakfast, and I was feeling hungry. We decided to stop for lunch on the walk back to the hotel. The sky had become cloudy and grey. It looked as though it was about to rain. By lunchtime, we were tired and hungry, so we decided to stop at a small French café for lunch. It had started to rain, so we asked for a table inside.

As soon as we were seated, I noticed a lovely woman sitting at a table next to us. She was sitting with a much younger man who had features very similar to hers. I assumed he was her son because of their strong resemblance. They were a very striking pair, and for some strange reason, they looked very familiar. They reminded me of my neighbors back home in Louisiana.

I was close enough to hear everything they were saying. Although they were speaking in French, I understood every word they said. I am fluent in French. I took courses in high school and college. I believed that learning foreign languages would be useful in the business world. I had been correct about that fact. On that day, it was helpful in a personal way.

They were discussing his news about an internship in America. He was so excited, but his mother was not at all excited. She had a worried look on her face, but he didn't notice. He was so involved in his conversation. She was trying her best to look supportive. I continued watching them from the corner of my eye for a long while.

I had a visceral reaction to the woman, and I could not stop myself from looking at her. My response began to frighten me. She was such a stunning woman, and she felt incredibly familiar. I began to feel a chill come over my body. I was having a difficult time breathing.

"Jazz, Paul's pet name for me, Are you okay? You look pale." He reached over and grabbed my hand.

"Her eyes, I was trying hard to remember where I had seen those brown eyes before. All of a sudden, I remembered why she seemed so familiar. They were the eyes of the woman in my picture; Nana had given me when I was a child. The eyes of my mother, I continued to ponder. I finally whispered to my husband, as tears began to roll down my face, "I am staring at the eyes of my mother!"

He knew I had to be mistaken, so it caused him to become deeply concerned.

Then the woman looked up from the conversation she was having with her son. The lovely lady spotted me starring at her and could not turn away either. At that moment, I knew for sure she was my mother!

"Oh my God, what on Earth will I do or say?" I thought. I tried to stand up, but I fainted into the arms of the love of my life, my new husband.

TWENTY-ONE

"Jazzy, my darling, wake up!" I recognized Paul's voice calling; he is the only one who calls me that. It sounded like it was coming from far away. His voice sounded muffled.

"Jazmine, Jazmine, please wake up honey," I heard a woman's voice say.

My grandmother had always called me Jazmine. She never liked my nickname, but she was dead so that it couldn't be her voice. Sometimes, when Nana was upset with me, she would call me by my full name. "Jazmine Walton, where are you, young lady?" Nana would call out. However, the woman's voice I heard was calling my name with a French accent. I finally opened my eyes and felt as though I had awakened from a bad dream.

When I opened my eyes, Paul asked me, "Are you feeling okay, baby?" He was still holding me in his arms, because I had just fainted. The lovely woman was standing next to him. Her face was very familiar. For a moment, I thought I was back in New Orleans. After she called my name, she asked me if I was okay. Then reality struck, and I remembered what caused me to faint. I looked at her, long and hard, in disbelief. Then she said, "Hello, my dear. I am your mother."

I shook my head in disbelief and fainted again. I had never fainted before in my entire life, but this morning I had fainted twice before lunch. I skipped breakfast that morning and drank a lot of champagne the night before, so I thought maybe that was the problem.

After the second time, I became alert and recognized an emergency medical tech checking my blood pressure. I was healthy, the tech announced, but nothing else was at that moment. I was both shocked and confused.

This time, I turned my head and stared at the face of my deceased mother. However, she was alive and living in Paris! I slowly started to remember that we were in a restaurant in Paris on my honeymoon.

How could she be standing here? Many questions began to formulate in my mind, but at the moment, I could not articulate any words.

Finally, I asked her, "Are you, really my mother? I thought you were dead"

"Yes, I am my dear."

"How is that possible? Your parents told my dad, you died when you were on a trip. What are you doing here, in Paris? Is that young man you were with my brother?"

"Yes, he is your brother. His name is Philip, and he does not know anything about my past."

"If you feel strong enough to stand up, we should leave this restaurant, and find a quiet place to talk. I would like to explain to you why I had to leave you and your father."

Paul was dumbfounded by what he was witnessing, and finally spoke up and said, "Our hotel is very close, so maybe we should go there. Are you sure about walking back?"

I said, "I feel fine. I believe the hotel lobby would be a satisfactory place for me to have a conversation with my mother."

At that moment, I became angry with my father because he had lied to me about my mother all my life or some reason, I didn't blame Nana because I am sure she must have been forced by my father to keep this secret. I know that Nana would have never done anything to cause me pain because she loved me too much.

For the majority of my life, Daddy had been a cold, unhappy man. However, he and my newly resurrected mother had some serious explaining to do. The three of us walked back to our hotel less than a block away. Phillip had a previous engagement and left soon after I fainted. Paul suggested that he wait for me at the bar. He left me with the woman who claimed to be my mother, so we could be alone to talk. I am positive my husband called his father-in-law, as soon as he was out of earshot. However, I was not concerned about Daddy at that moment.

TWENTY-TWO

I began to question the woman who said she was my mother. "What is your name? Do you live here, in Paris? Most of all, why are you here?"

"My name is Olivia Swayne, and I own a home in the countryside nearby. I have been living here since I was eighteen years old. How did you recognize me?" She inquired.

I told her that I recognized her face from an old picture Nana had given me when I was a child. "My father never talked about you. He told me that you were dead and seemed sad whenever I tried to broach the subject."

The next thing she said was," I want you to know that I have always loved you, and leaving you was the most challenging thing I have ever done. I have a cousin back in Louisiana that sends me updates on your life. I also know that you recently married that young man you were with at the restaurant, but she didn't know where the two of you were going on your honeymoon. I had no clue you were in Paris. It was a coincidence that we ended up at the same cafe. Our meeting today is destiny, and there was no way of preventing it from happening.

I do not want you to blame Walton. She called Daddy by his given name. He doesn't know that I am alive. Your grandmother did not know the truth either."

In the meantime, Paul was informing Daddy that a woman in Paris was claiming to be my mother. He listened intently to what my husband had to say. Then my father started taking deep breaths. His chest was starting to hurt, and the intake of air helped him calm down. He believed that Paul was telling him the truth.

All my father managed to say was: "I don't know what is happening. If this is true, I know Jazmine well enough to believe that she will be angry and hurt."

Paul said, "We have plans to return Louisiana in a few days. Mr. Walton, I don't

126

have a clue about what you are planning to do, but you should start working on it immediately. I think my wife might need you close right now. She seems lost and confused."

My father hung up the phone. He called for his secretary to make reservations for a first-class flight to Paris as soon as possible. Daddy wanted to be there to tell me his side of this horrible story, if he didn't have a massive coronary first.

My mother continued her story: "Your father and I were very much in love. My parents were aware of your grandfather's affair with his secretary. They also knew that he had abandoned him and Nana when your father was young. They did not like him and did not believe he was good enough for their daughter.

When I was eighteen, I got pregnant the night of his senior prom. My father refused to allow me to see Walton again. At the beginning of our summer break that year, they planned a short vacation to France. Walton had gone away to football camp, and I was excited about my first trip to Europe. I had not discussed the pregnancy with him yet, and I was a little anxious about telling him.

The trip was just a ruse; my parents had enrolled me into a rigorous, religious, boarding school. It was on the outskirts of Paris. You were immediately adopted after you were born. They refused to tell your father where I was and eventually told him that I was dead.

Somehow your grandmother found out about the pregnancy. She hired a detective to find the baby, you Jazmine. Nana brought back to Louisiana. She also thought I was dead.

My parents agreed to keep their elaborate story that I was dead. I never saw them again. I never spoke with Walton again, and never returned to Louisiana. My parents died in a car accident soon after I graduated from a boarding school in Paris. They were rich and left me a hefty inheritance and had a trust created for you also. I understand that you used the money to start an advertising firm in Atlanta, Georgia. I know that you are quite successful. It was easier for everyone to believe that I was dead, I thought.

I got married in my thirties, to a much older man, and we had our son Philip. He died several years ago."

"That scenario was great for everyone involved except poor little Jazmine, I stated bitterly. How could you do something like that to your firstborn child? What kind of a monster does a thing like that?

I blame you for keeping this vital information from us. I had the right to know the truth! I am so angry with you. I can't think straight! I don't want to talk about this anymore today! Maybe we can discuss this situation more tomorrow.

I would eventually like to meet my brother, Phillip. I will allow you all the time you need to explain everything to him, just let me know when you are ready. He will have a chance to see what kind of mother you are."

"Let me know when you are ready, but in the meantime, Jazmine, please don't be angry with your father. Walton thought that I was dead, and Nana did also. She always wanted to protect both of you." Olivia requested.

"Angry? I don't feel anything now except hurt! I can't describe the pain I am feeling right now! All my life, my dad was too bitter and hurt even to call your name. I blame you for his pain.

I missed having a mother so much. I wondered about what it would be like to have you in my life. Nana gave me an old picture of you, Olivia. I looked at your picture every night after saying my prayers, but you were not dead, you're alive. Now you are standing there trying to convince me that you were doing what was best, but you were doing what was best for you! Now, I am ready to find my husband. After all we are here on our honeymoon!"

TWENTY-THREE

Daddy arrived in Paris the following evening. Paul had informed me that he was on the way. I made arrangements with Olivia to meet us at the restaurant in the hotel. The day before, I explained to my mother that I needed time the process what had happened to me. I hope she understood how much all of this had affected me.

I was sitting facing the door of the restaurant. I glanced up as Daddy walked into the place. He didn't notice me at first. His focus was on the woman.

Olivia's back was to the door when he entered. My dad began to walk towards our table. As he slowly started toward us, I could see tears in his eyes. I had never seen him cry before, even at my grandmother's funeral. He looked as though he was in a trance. She turned around to see who I was staring. Daddy walked straight toward her.

The look on his face touched my heart. I glanced over at my mother, and she had the same look in her eyes. They were both crying.

Olivia stood up as he approached, and then they embraced for a long time. Not a word was passed between the two of them, as they just stood there holding each other. I realized, at that moment, they had a profound love for each other.

Finally, I believed the story Olivia had told me the previous day. I could feel the love they shared that created me. How much pain had they endured all the years they were forced to be apart?

Finally, he came over, kissed on my cheek, and asked, "How are you holding up, my dear?"

"I am in a state of shock!"

He nodded a greeting to Paul, then sat down, and exclaimed, "I need a stiff drink."

He ordered a Jack Daniels with Coca-Cola. I ordered a glass of wine, and so did my mother. The first words my father manage to ask my mother was, "Olivia, I thought you were dead! How on Earth is it possible for you to be alive?"

Her response was, "I am happy to see you. It will take a long time to explain all of it to you, my love. First, I think we should order dinner. Afterward Walton, I promise I will explain everything to you."

We ordered Coq Au Vin, small roasted potatoes with pearl onions, and a fresh vegetable medley. Our dinner was family-style.

I didn't eat very much, and neither did my mother. Paul and Daddy ate like it was their last supper; they enjoyed the meal.

My husband and I decided to skip dessert because it was plain to see my mother and father needed to begin a discussion without our presence. We announced that we were going for a walk in the moonlight.

As we began our stroll, Paul said that when he talked to my father, the previous morning, he got the impression that he was not aware that my mother was alive. After my father walked over to the table, Paul said he was sure that Daddy was telling the truth as we began to stroll. I saw the look on your mother's face. She had the look of a forlorn girl, as she glanced at her lover.

My husband and I went for a walk in the moonlight. Our hotel was very close to the Eiffel Tower, so we headed in that direction. Every morning we had our coffee on the balcony, and enjoyed with a view of it in the daylight. Seeing it all lit up at night was awe inspiring. We only had a few days of our honeymoon left, so we agreed to go sightseeing in the next day.

When we first arrived in Paris, the architecture reminded me of southern Louisiana, but it was city was pristine. I didn't see any trash on the streets. The lawns were perfectly manicured.

He put his arm around my shoulder as we walked and asked me, "Baby, you've been very quiet tonight. How are you feeling about all this?"

"I am still shocked and confused. But as I watched the two of them across the table from each other, holding hand, it was clear that they love each other. It is easier for me to believe my mother's explanation now.

Do you remember the first night, we danced together, at that popular night club back home? I tried to explain to you how much I longed to see my mother. I think God granted my wish yesterday.

We are here to enjoy our honeymoon, so let's just try our best to enjoy the trip."

TWENTY-FOUR

"**W**alton, it is so wonderful to see you," my mother began as soon as they were alone.

"It is wonderful to see you again also, Olivia, but I need you to explain to me how this is possible."

"I understand how you feel. I got pregnant that night after the prom. It was our first time, and our protection failed to work correctly. A few weeks later, my mother took me to see a doctor, and we received the results. My parents did not believe in abortion, and I didn't either. I wanted to tell you, so I tried calling you, but you had already gone away to football camp. I desperately needed to discuss it with you. I wasn't sure how you would feel about the pregnancy. You had been so excited about your football scholarship.

When school was out for the summer, my parents wanted me to go along with them to Europe. I was excited about the trip, so we flew to France, but it was all a ruse! My parents had arranged for me to stay at a strict religious boarding school until the baby was born. I never had a chance even to hold her.

By that time, you had already started your college freshman year. I was sure you hated me, so I agreed with my parents that adoption was the best thing for my child. Soon after she was born, I started college here, France, and have remained here until now. After the baby was born, I planned to come back home, but my parents told me that you were engaged. At that point, I felt nothing was left back home for me, so I never turned to Louisiana. My parents were killed in a crash, soon after I started college, in Paris. I didn't attend the memorial service either. Since they had tricked me, I blamed them for all my misery. For years, I mourned the loss of my child. I also missed you and the love we shared. I thought about both you often.

Soon after I started my career, I met my husband. He was much older than I, and he was a patient and kind man. He was a member of a large family, and they welcomed me into their fold. We only had one child, Philip. He just accepted an internship in California at a sports agency."

After Olivia explained, Daddy checked into the hotel, where we were staying.

He did not immediately use it; the two of them walked and talked for most of the night.

By morning my mother had returned home. My father tried to get some rest; neither of them had been able to sleep. They were so excited to be back in each other's lives.

When they met again the following morning, Olivia exclaimed: "I hired a detective to search for my child; I only knew that my parents arranged the adoption somewhere in the south. That was the only information I was able to give to the detective. I was shocked, when I discovered that you and Nana were raising my daughter."

She commented, Walton, you and Nana did an excellent job raising Jazmine. "I always liked your mother. Thank God she was there to save the day." She is beautiful, and seems enamored with her husband."

"Yes, they are very much in love." They have known each other since she finished high school, but they were on different paths for over a decade. Somehow, they got back together again."

"Your parents told me you were dead, and told you I got engaged after I left for college. I was never engaged. Your parents lied to keep us apart. What a cruel thing to do to a person you are supposed to love. In the end, they were not able to keep us apart, and we also have a lovely daughter."

"I called and asked her to meet for lunch tomorrow. Afterward, I want the two of us to have a long talk. I totally understand why she is angry; she has every right to be. All those years, she was denied a life with me, because of my parents. I want her to know how much I love her."

"Yes, and I have been trying to make up for all the grief I caused her, for several years. I was so bitter and hurt. She deserved so much better. Her grandmother tried to provide all the love she needed. She knew Jazmine needed her for love and support."

"Walton, why didn't you ever marry?"

"Because, I never found the kind of love we shared. For the majority of my younger years, I was too bitter to share my life with anyone. I met someone a few years before Nana died. She was a retired kindergarten teacher. I grew to love her. She died from breast cancer. Following her death, I never had another relationship. That's enough talk for now. Please sit by me, so that I can hold you. I have wanted to do that all evening. We have a lot of lost time to makeup.

What would you like to get from room service? If you prefer, we can go downstairs to one of the hotel's restaurants"

"I have an idea. How about we skip the food and go straight to dessert?" She smiled and fluttered her long eyelashes.

His reply was, "Darling that is a wonderful idea. I love the way your mind works."

TWENTY-FIVE

"**J**azz darling, what would you like for breakfast? I will order room service, and we can have breakfast in bed."

"I'm still tired from yesterday. I don't think I've ever walked that much before in one day. How about we rest in bed after breakfast and later shower together?"

"That sounds like a winner," He said as he winked at me.

Then, I thought about the conversation I had with Olivia. I was about to have a lunch date with my mother and father today. I felt nervous. I knew the night before, that they needed some time to talk and get reacquainted. Not realizing, at that time, they were getting well acquainted in his hotel room.

Olivia got up early and left Walton's hotel room. She returned to her home in order to dress for lunch. We agreed to meet at one o'clock in the small garden restaurant next to the hotel.

Paul and I stayed in bed until it was time to get dressed. It was a beautiful warm, sunny day, a wonderful time for having lunch outside.

My mother and father, were already waiting at the restaurant. We greeted each other and got comfortable on the patio of the fragrantly smelling restaurant. The menu had lots of tasty delicacies. I had no clue about what I wanted for lunch, so I decided to order the daily special.

After we finished eating our lunch, Olivia asked, "Jazmine, I would like for the two of us to spend a little time alone today. There is something I want to discuss with you, mother requested."

Daddy spoke up and said, "Paul and I have some business to discuss, since I will be staying here for a short vacation. Olivia has promised to show me all that Paris has to offer.

Are you ladies going shopping? Please take my AMX card and buy anything you need for dinner tomorrow night," Daddy, exclaimed gleefully.

"Thank you, my dear Walton, but I have my own American Express card. We will meet you guys later."

I glanced over at Paul; he smiled and nodded his head. It had been one hell of a honeymoon. I am sure he was thinking. I will have the rest of my life to make it up to him.

As we strolled through a park across the street, Olivia began her conversation. "First of all, Jazmine, I want you to know that I love you and I always have. I realize allowing my parents to take you and give you to someone for adoption was a cowardly thing to do. I should have fought harder. I tried to reach out to Walton several times to no avail.

After I graduated from college, I found a job here in Paris, so I made this city my home. I also waited too long to hire someone to search for you. Once I found out you were safe and happy with your father and grandmother, I was shocked to discover that my parents arranged your adoption with

Nana. I am so sorry that I missed all of the special occasions of your life. I should have been there for your birthday, school plays, and speeches. I am incredibly sorry about missing your graduation. Even though I wasn't there for you, please know, I never stopped thinking about you or your father.

I understand if you don't want me anywhere near you or your family. It is what I deserve. Instead of giving me a chance, I will try my best to prove how much I care. I love both of you so much, and I would like to share some small part of your life.

I want you to know that your father is trying to persuade me to return to Louisiana to live with him. I have given it a lot of thought. My answer depends on your opinion about this idea. I want to know how you feel about your father and me seeing each other again. It has been a whirlwind for you. I am sure you never expected anything like this to happen on your honeymoon."

"Olivia, I want whatever is best for my dad. If that means sharing his life with you, I'm okay with you returning to Louisiana with him."

"I am so sorry. I was so young and had no money of my own. I could not come back to the United States without help from my parents. They did not care for Walton and did everything they could to keep us apart. I was not in the position to take care of a child, and my parents convinced me that your father no longer wanted a relationship. I was so miserable and broken-hearted. I was sure that adoption was my only option."

"I know my father is willing to forgive you, but I am trying my best to understand. I can see how difficult it must have been to be a teenager so far away from home. It must have been challenging to be eighteen, pregnant, and alone.

When I was a child, I wanted so desperately to know things about you. Nana gave me a picture of you because I was always questioning Daddy. He would never answer me because he believed you rejected him. Would you like to see the picture? I carry it with me in my wallet."

"Thank you; I would love to see the photograph."

As she held it in her hand, tears began to well in her eyes, she said softly, "Walton took this picture of me the summer before my senior year. It was the most joyous summer of my life. I loved your father so much, and he loved me in return. I haven't given your father my answer yet. I wanted to talk to you first.

I have to remain in Europe until Phillip's graduation in London. The ceremony will be in a couple of weeks. I plan to spend the weekend with him and try to explain my past to him; he deserves to hear the story from me.

After Philip graduates, he will be moving to California. He has an internship in Los Angles for six months. It would be great for both of us to be living in America at the same time, but only if he understands and accepts my explanation. He is a kind and loving soul, and I am proud of him. I believe that once he gets to know you, he will love you as his big sister.

I wanted to have this talk with you first, before our dinner party tomorrow night. I will give Walton my answer after dinner. If I decide to move back home, I think it would be best to find a small place of my own while we become reacquainted. I wanted to have your approval first. I hope that you will forgive me and allow me to get to know you better and share a small part of your life."

"I think that is a good idea, but Daddy will not agree. I have never seen him happier then he has been since he arrived in Paris. Observing the way he smiles when he looks at you, I feel that it would bring him so much joy if you moved back."

"Walton brings me joy also. For many years, I believed that he hated me. I thought that he had moved on with his life. Thank you, Jazmine, for giving us a second chance. I love your father with all my heart. I loved him even before I knew what the word love meant. Life has given Walton and me another chance to be together again."

TWENTY-SIX

"Jazmine, how would you like to go shopping? I need to buy some things for our small gathering tomorrow night." Olivia said.

"Sure that sounds like a fun idea, I love to shop. I haven't had a chance to do much shopping since we arrived.

Paul doesn't care much for it, but he goes along sometimes anyway to make me happy. We are leaving in a couple of days. Let's go to that giant mall; I have heard so much about since we got here. I need to buy as many beautiful items as I can find, before we go back home."

This was my first trip to the enormous, popular mall. It was a short distance from our hotel. It had majestic stained glass ceilings, and all the floors on every level were made of glass. Each floor was dedicated to certain departments. I especially liked the floor entirely dedicated to glamour shoes.

I know my grandmother would have loved shopping here. I felt a little sad thinking about her. She had only been gone for a year. Even though I was on my honeymoon, I missed her so much. I know she would be pleased that I had married my wonderful husband. She liked him very much when we were young, and wanted us to be together.

I bought him a watch from Cartier's, for a honeymoon gift. He loved watches and wore one every day. Olivia and I bought new dresses to wear at her dinner party the following evening."

One floor of the mall was dedicated totally for housewares. She purchased several matching items for the party. She had them delivered to her house.

On our walk back to the hotel, we stopped at a bakery called, "Blossoms," There was a large circular glass case filled with delicious pastries. Olivia said they were famous for their macaroons. They were supposed to be the best ones in Paris. She ordered two dozen of those.

While we waited, we shared cups of coffee. As we waited on our order in the quaint little place, Olivia said, "Your father and I attended the same Catholic school. I had a crush on him starting my freshman year of high school. He was a grade higher than me, and Walton was our star, football quarterback. He was amazing to watch, but he never noticed me until the summer before his senior year. He asked me if I wanted to accompany him to a summer pool party. I answered yes, and we were inseparable after that night. I guess we have continued to love each other since then."

I felt genuinely happy that she and Daddy had been reunited. It was wonderful to believe that he had found his soul mate, and finally had joy in his life. I know his mother would be happy that her grumpy, brooding son had finally found his true love. I thought about how disappointed she would be with me for holding a grudge against my mother. For the first time my feelings for Olivia began to soften a little.

She changed to another subject. She started talking about her garden, and in turn I described Nana's gardens to her. She told me that we would be dining on her patio under the evening sky. Before we left the bakery, she also ordered, dozens of tea cakes, and petit fours.

Olivia also told me that she hired a personal chef to prepare the food for the party. I could hear the excitement in her voice about the party, she was planning for us.

TWENTY-SEVEN

After my shopping trip with Olivia, I returned to our hotel suite. The sun was just beginning to set. Paul was sitting on the balcony enjoying the view. I walked over to him, sat on his lap. I wrapped my arms around him, as soon as I sat down, it was apparent that he had missed his wife very much. He gently lifted me up and carried me to the king-sized bed of our honeymoon suite.

Then, he reminded me of how much he loved me. At first, his kisses were gentle but soon became much more intense, as we swiftly removed clothes

Hours later, equally satisfied, we ordered dinner from room service. We enjoyed our meal in our cozy hotel bathrobes. After eating, my husband gently slipped his hands into my robe, slid it off my shoulders, and allowed it to drop to the floor. He began to nibble and taste as though I was the best dessert he had ever devoured. When he finished, he lifted my limp body. I felt like a wilted flower. I was unable to move any part of my body. He carried me to a warm bubble bath, in a luxurious claw foot tub, then joined me in the tub. We soaked in that tub until the water became cool. We towel dried our bodies and headed back to the bed. In his arms, I felt as though the chaos that had transpired no longer existed. We immediately drifted off to a peaceful night's sleep.

The next morning, as the sunlight was streaming through our balcony doors, I awakened to my beautiful husband gazing at me like a child on Christmas morning waiting to open his gift. Slowly I began to realize that I was his gift. His warm, gentle hands found their way down my body from my breast to the soft, hot space between my thighs. He slowly opened his present.

After our passionate lovemaking, we ordered breakfast. We decided to remain in bed. It was the last day of our honeymoon. We connected on a deeper level as we discussed our future together. We stayed there until it was time to dress for Olivia's dinner party in the French Countryside. She wanted us to meet a small group of her friends.

When we arrived, there were three couples in the living room. They were drinking wine and discussing politics. My father answered the door when we got there.

He said, "Please come in as he welcomed us into the house."

He was smiling brightly and looked very happy. My mother was impeccably dressed when we arrived at her house. I was impressed with the lovely jewelry she wore. Usually, I wear silver hoops or the large gold ones that my father gave me for a graduation gift. For the party that night, I wore Nana's lovely pearl necklace and matching earrings as well as the dress I brought from the mall the previous day. It was a lovely lightweight silk floral print dress.

Paul was dressed in a lightweight linen jacket, jeans, and a light blue shirt. He looked as handsome as always.

"Hello, Olivia said. I see you are wearing the watch that Jazmine bought for you yesterday." She remarked to Paul.

"He smiled and said, "My wife has excellent taste."

"Thank you for coming," she said and kissed us on both cheeks. That seemed to be the way everybody greeted in France. "Would you like something to drink," she asked.

Paul asked for sparkling water with lemon or lime, and I asked for a glass of wine. Daddy looked at home as he poured my glass of wine. Olivia went into the kitchen to get my husband's drink. After returning, she announced that dinner would be ready in ten minutes. We made ourselves comfortable, and in the meantime, she introduced us to all her friends.

I spotted my father talking with her invited guest as though he was a host at the party. As she stepped through the door ahead of us, my dad lifted his eyes to hers and his face lit up with joy. He had had been that way ever since he arrived in Paris. For the first time, I could feel their passionate, adoring, and unconditional love they felt for each other her. At that moment, I could tell that they would never be torn apart again.

Olivia's home was very large and beautifully decorated. I had imagined she lived in a small cottage, but this place was immense. It had six bedrooms and five bathrooms. Beyond her expansive French doors, was a well-lit portico surrounded by a beautiful flower garden. In the middle of the yard was a large water feature with a statue of a cherub with wings. The water was flowing from his hands. There were candles and white twinkling lights everywhere. The backyard was enclosed with a high brick fence painted white. Our dinner party was on a large table, on her patio. The garden was lovely, and the lawn was beautiful. It was a warm, starry night, and I felt a pleasant, soft breeze. We shared some wine on her patio.

A private chef had prepared the food and hired a waiter staff to serve our meal. The dinner started with a green salad and a light vinaigrette dressing. For the main course, we were served perfectly grilled rack of lamb, with roasted summer vegetables and creaming cheesy potatoes. For dessert, we had the choice of a featherweight lemon cake, or the incredible macaroons from Blossoms, the French bakery we visited the previous day.

It was a pleasant spring night, and I felt very pleased. After dinner, we enjoyed more wine on the patio. The party was terrific, but Paul and I had an early morning flight. We needed to end our evening early and return to the hotel.

I hugged my mother for the first time and said goodbye. "I hope you have decided to come back to the states," I whispered in her ear.

"Yes, I think I have. I will tell your father tonight after the party," she told me as we were leaving the party.

Olivia had been planning to give him an answer, about moving back to Louisiana, after all her guests had gone. After the party ended, she said, "Walton I have given your invitation, to return to the States, a lot of thought. There is nothing I would like better, but I have to stay in Europe for a few more weeks.

Phillip is graduating from college, in two weeks. I must be present. It is in London. I plan to stay there overnight and explain all of this to my son. I pray he will understand and find forgiveness in his heart. He is one of the sweetest and most loving persons I know. I love him very much. Phillip will be leaving for California after his graduation. After that, my darling, I will come to Louisiana and all my time will be yours."

"Olivia, darling, please know that I want nothing more than to take you home with me. I totally understand, and if it is okay with you, I would like to stay here with you for another week. I have decided to take a much-needed vacation. Paul can handle the business until my return. He will run my company, when I retire, but I have not announced it yet.

I hope that all goes well with you and Phillip. I look forward to seeing you back in our hometown very soon."

The following morning my mother and father were there to see us off. We said goodbye in front of the hotel while the limo driver loaded our luggage into the vehicle.

Daddy announced: "I think I will stay in Paris for a few more days. I will be home soon. Thanks for offering to take a commercial flight. I love you so much."

My father had flown to Paris on the red-eye. We flew to Paris on his company's private plane, a Gulfstream. Since he decided to remain in France for a few more days, his secretary booked us a first-class flight home. We only had to agree to stay in Paris an extra day. That was fine with us. A limo was scheduled to pick us up very early Sunday morning.

Since Daddy was not sure exactly when he would be ready to fly home, we wanted him to come back on his plane. It was secure in a hanger, and his pilot on standby.

Paul volunteered to take care of his company until he was ready to come home. He said it would be no longer than a week at the most.

Maybe he would be able to persuade Olivia to come back with him, but in the meantime, they had a lot of catching up to do.

"I love you too, Daddy."

"Have a safe trip back. I will see you guys very soon."

"Okay, Mr. Walton, I'll take care of everything at work. You need a vacation, so you don't have to rush back. If a problem arises, I will call you, so take your time, and come home whenever you're ready."

"I trust your judgment, son. Feel free to call me anytime. If you need answers to any questions, I will be available."

TWENTY-EIGHT

As soon as we were comfortable in our seats, we fell asleep. We were exhausted, but it had been a wonderfully exciting honeymoon.

I began to dream about Nana. I was sitting on her back porch. There were four white rocking chairs with floral pads on them for comfort. There was also a ceiling fan, and it stayed on throughout the day. This place was my grandmother's sanctuary. She spent the majority of her free time talking with me, or her friends, always with a smile on her face.

"Jazmine Walton, she was calling, I am not going to call you again. I have called you three times. It is time for you to come inside for dinner."

She never called me Jazzy, but whenever she called me by my full name, I knew she meant business. I had never challenged Nana's authority, because of the love and respect I felt for her. When I was a young child she was the closest thing to a mother that anyone could ask for, but she wasn't. She was much older than all of the other mothers.

I didn't notice a difference until I reached Middle School. It became obvious that I was different. I began to wish for the same type of relationship my friends had with their mothers. My feelings changed in high school. My friends thought that I had the coolest grandmother. They enjoyed coming to our house for sleepovers on the weekend. Nana was never overbearing; she allowed us all the space we needed to have fun. She took care of everyone's needs and prepared all our favorite foods. Having her around was like having our own private chef.

By the summer of my 16th birthday, I started to see her in a different light. I think it was because I had finally matured enough to realize how blessed I was to have such a wonderful grandmother. From that point, my love for her grew even more. We became inseparable.

During my dream, I could see myself sitting in her favorite rocking chair. My father and I had to plan her funeral.

As I continued to rock, I heard her voice say, "Jazmine, it is time for you to forgive your mother. Both of you have suffered too much. Now, I want you to give her a chance to love you."

Our plane experienced turbulence, and I woke up with a start. I reached for my husband's hand.

He said, "Jazzy, you have been talking in your sleep."

"Yes, I was talking to Nana," I mumbled, and went back to sleep. If someone said they were talking to a deceased person, it would sound strange. But he loved me enough to understand that I was still missing my grandmother.

The next time I woke up, the flight attendant was serving dinner. I asked for a glass of wine. We were almost home. I felt relaxed and at peace.

TWENTY-NINE

Phillip said, "Hey Mom. Graduation lasted a lot longer than I anticipated. I'm glad it's over now. I have my diploma, and I am excited to be moving to California."

"I am happy too, Philip. Let's go grab some lunch."

"That's fine, Mom, but first, I would like to say goodbye to some of my friends. Is that okay with you? I am leaving London on the red-eye tonight."

"Sure darling, go right ahead, I will wait right here until you are ready to leave."

"Thanks, Mommy, I'll be right back."

"He hasn't called me that in years," she thought, as he rushed over to his friends.

Olivia was anxious about how Phillip would receive the information about her past, but she had to tell him the truth.

When Philip finished saying goodbye to his friends, he took off his cap and gown. "Mom, I am ready to go now. We can go to this cafe near the campus. Everyone has been talking about how good the food is there. Would you like to go check it out?"

"Sure, honey. Any place we eat is fine with me."

"Mom, you look worried. What's going on, are you sick or something?" Phillip asked.

"No, I am not sick. I feel wonderful. I was encouraged to see you march across that stage. I know how anxious you are to begin the next chapter of your life. I am so very proud of you!"

After they ordered lunch, Olivia took a deep breath and said, "Phillip, I have something I need to tell you. She started with a question. Do you remember that young woman that fainted at the café, the day you left to return to London?"

"Vaguely, I remember telling you the news about my internship in America. After that, I had to rush off to catch my flight back to London. Why are you asking?"

After Phillip quietly listened to her entire story, without interruption, he stood up and gave her a big hug. As tears rolled down her face, she sighed, "I am so ashamed and sorry about all of this."

"It is okay, Mom, there is no need to feel ashamed. You had a tough time all alone in a foreign country. You survived a lot, so you should be proud of yourself! You are a powerful woman. I love you very much.

Do you want to go back to where you grew up? If you do, we will both be in America, and we can see each other more."

"Yes, I am excited to return after all these years. I plan to find a place to live and stay in Louisiana for a while."

"I am happy and amazed that the young woman from the restaurant, is my older sister. I can't wait to meet her. When are you leaving the house in Paris?"

"I have plans to leave at the end of this week," Olivia replied.

THIRTY

After weeks of communicating every day by email, Facetime, and Skype, Olivia joined her loving Walton in their home town. She was finally back in the place where she was born. Even though she checked into a suite at a hotel downtown, she spent the majority of her time at my father's house. He was not happy about it, but he accompanied her along with a realtor to search for a new townhouse or condo. He went along begrudgingly, secretly hoping she wouldn't find a place that satisfied her.

Mother had moved back to her home town. My father wanted to plan a party for her to celebrate. He was excited about her returning, so he asked me to help with the plans. He decided to invite all her old friends, as well as our family and neighbors. I invited Arden and Ashley to come from Atlanta for the special night.

Keeping the party arrangements from Olivia was a daunting task. Daddy had sworn us all to secrecy. Even Phillip was included in his plan.

The party was a hit. Olivia was surprised, and her Walton seemed to be on top of the world. He was so excited. He pulled out all the stops.

The event was held in an enormous white silk tent in our back yard. There hung a beautiful chandelier in the middle. Tiny white lights adorned the entire tent.

After a short while had passed, and daddy had indulged in a couple of glasses of Jack Daniels, he asked everyone to join him in a toast. Then he shocked us all.

"To my darling Olivia welcome home!" After every one finished their drinks, he reached into his jacket pocket. He pulled out small black box as he started to bend on one knee.

"Olivia, I have loved you for as long as I can remember. Will you accept my proposal to spend the rest of your life as my wife?"

"Oh, my Darling Walton, I would like nothing better. I love you more than words can say. Now honey, do you think you need any help getting off your knee? Everyone laughed, then cheered and said, "A toast to the happy couple."

The ring was one of the most beautiful pieces of jewelry I had ever seen. It had a very large princess cut diamond in the center of two baguettes on each side and smaller begets around the entire band. It fit her finger perfectly, as he slid it onto her ring finger. Olivia's face was glowing. There was no doubt in my mind that she also loved him unconditionally also. It had been their destiny to find each other once again.

I felt so much joy for them at that moment. I reached up and wrapped my arms around Paul's neck, pulled his face down close for a passionate kiss.

He asked: "What was that for, Jazzy? Don't get me wrong, I'm not complaining by any means."

"It was just because I know I can whenever I feel like it, and because I love you so much!"

"In that case, maybe we should try that again."

Since Olivia's birthday followed her arrival back to Louisiana that was the day she chose for her wedding. It was a warm, sunny, spring day and totally awesome for a wedding. We held it in Nana's flower garden. I am sure she was smiling down on us. She always enjoyed a happy ending.

I was the maid of honor and Paul was the best man. He stood next to my father under a floral, bridal arch. I watched intently as I slowly walked toward them. Of course, my husband was wearing his killer smile, and that always caused me to melt inside.

I joined them and turned around to face the bride, as she slowly walked toward my father. He actually cried. That was an incredible thing for me to witness. As I watched them share their vows, l knew that the love they shared had created me, and nothing in this universe could keep them apart.

After the wedding, we had a small catered reception in the house. "Please raise a glass for a toast to the happy couple, my mother, and father. Congratulations to both of you. We wish you many years of happiness.

Olivia had finally moved in with Daddy. She had made a few changes, but for the most part, she said Nana had excellent taste. It was a wonderful home.

Mr. and Mrs. James Walton decided to spend a long weekend in nearby New Orleans for their honeymoon.

When the reception had finally come to an end, I yawned and told Paul I was extremely tired. As we stood on the front porch and waved goodbye, to my newly wedded parents, I thought my life was just about perfect. "It doesn't get much better than this." I said softly to myself. I could not been more pleased than I was at that time in my life.

All of a sudden, I felt nauseous and light-headed at the same time. I wondered why I was feeling so ill. Then, I remembered my missed doctor's appointment. My period was a couple of months late. It had happened to me several times before, as a teenager, so I wasn't too overly concerned.

As my knees began to buckle, I collapsed into the arms of my strong, handsome, and virile husband. He looked at me and said: "Not again, Jazzy!"

THE END

EPILOGUE

Six months later, we were blessed with beautiful twin girls. We named the firstborn Christina. Nana's name was Christine. The second baby was named Olivia for my mother. I have forgiven my mother for the past. We have become very close over the last couple of years.

When my father retired, Paul became the CEO. I barely recognize my father. He has become a warm, loving, agreeable man. Mom and Dad have promised, to always be available to babysit the girls when needed.

Arden and Ashley are controlling both agencies in Texas and Atlanta. They want me to enjoy an extended maternity leave. "Jazzy, worrying about anything else except those babies is counterproductive," Arden explained. They assured me that they have everything under control.

Paul was over the moon about the birth of his daughters. My kind-hearted, loving husband was just like his deceased, Papa. He will be one of the best fathers on Earth. I feel so blessed to have all of this love in my life!

ABOUT THE AUTHOR

Carla Stewart, Ed. S is a retired educator. She is a native of Mississippi, but has made the Atlanta, GA suburbs her home. She is the mother of two sons. She started writing as a hobby and after retiring, and joined a writer's class at a senior center.

She is a proud member of the Lou Walker Writer's Guild. She has published short stories and poetry published in two anthologies with the writer's guild; "Age Isn't Nothin but a Number" and "Sea of Life." This is her first novel.

Made in the USA
Las Vegas, NV
12 April 2021